A CUNNING DEATH

BLYTHE BAKER

Deceit and death in the country...

When Rose Beckingham receives a threatening message from a shadowy figure of the criminal underworld, she's forced to face her greatest fear--the exposure of all her secrets.

Forced to do the bidding of the man who calls himself the Chess Master, Rose accompanies Lord and Lady Ashton to their country estate and tries to thwart a murder before it happens.

With the Chess Master watching her every move and the brilliant French detective, Achilles Prideaux, dragging the deeds of her past out of the shadows, can Rose capture a killer in time to protect everyone she loves? Or will a weekend at Ridgewick Hall end the same way it began – with bloodshed?

1

First, I heard nothing. Then, slowly, a tinny ringing grew louder and louder until my entire body vibrated with it. I blinked against the gray haze in front of me, wondering whether I was somehow underwater. My chest felt impossibly heavy and it took several strong gasps before I could swallow any air. Each breath was acrid and ashy, burning my esophagus and scorching my lungs. I leaned forward, trying to get away from the fumes, and my face hit something solid. I reached for it and felt the hot leather upholstery of the front seat of the car.

Suddenly, everything came back to me all at once. The Beckinghams sharing the front seat with their driver, while Rose and I claimed the back. We were in Simla. At least, we had been...

Had I fallen asleep? That must have been it. I'd fallen asleep on the drive and was having a nightmare. I blinked hard in an attempt to wake myself up, but it didn't work. The smoke made my eyes water and I could feel tears streaming down my dusty cheeks.

"Rose?" I called, sliding my hand across the seat in search of my friend. "Mrs. Beckingham? Mr. Beckingham?"

I listened for their voices, but I couldn't hear anything aside from the sizzle of a nearby fire and the sound of someone coughing. Me. I was coughing.

"We will get you out, miss!"

There. Someone could hear me. I looked towards the direction of the voice and saw daylight streaming through what must have been the car window. Smoke and dust didn't allow me to see very far, but I could see human shapes moving around the vehicle.

Again, a flash of memory. A man moving through the crowd, arm pulled behind his head, a scowl on his face. The crowded streets near the market place pressed against our car, making it almost impossible to distinguish individual people from the mass, but this man had made himself obvious. He'd jumped around people, dodging arms and legs as he headed straight for us. I'd watched him with a curious eye, but didn't notice anything amiss until he swung his arm forward and released something.

With all the force of the initial blast, the horrifying truth came back to me.

Mrs. Beckingham gave a small yelp as the device landed inside the vehicle, Mr. Beckingham began to reach for it, Rose turned towards the commotion. My eyes, however, never left the man who had thrown the explosive. I watched as, content that his mission had been completed, he turned away from the car and disappeared back into the crowd. Then, darkness.

"Rose?" I shouted again, louder this time. "Answer me, Rose."

The car door opened, and a sticky breeze rolled through the opening, dispersing some of the smoke. It was as though someone had pulled back a curtain. I could see the seat in front of me, gouged and dripping with something sticky. I didn't linger on the sight, turning instead to where Rose had been sitting only a few minutes before. The seat was empty.

I could hear the sharp sounds of metal on metal coming from outside the car, and dusty silhouettes moved just outside the window. They were entreating me to calm down, to relax, to wait for help, but I leaned forward and swept my hand across the seat. I needed to find Rose.

Immediately, my hand landed in something warm and thick. I pulled back and held my hand up to the limited light coming through the door. Red dripped from my fingers, rolling down my wrist. I didn't need to think about what it was. I knew.

The contents of my stomach threatened to reappear, and I swallowed them down. I tried to take deep breaths, but the air was too thick. Everything felt wrong. The entire world had turned to chaos.

I looked back to where Rose should have been sitting, and for the first time, I saw something. A hand resting on the edge of the seat, as if Rose had simply slipped down to the floor between the front and back seats and was trying to pull herself back up.

I reached for her hand, wanting to help her, but in the brief second before our hands connected, I pulled back.

She wore a cheap metal ring with a fake jewel in the center. I'd bought it at a street market a few weeks before and had only recently given it to Rose. It was now the only thing that allowed me to identify the hand as hers, as it was no longer attached to her body. Where it should have connected to her arm, there was only mangled flesh and blood.

My mouth opened in a scream, but nothing came out. I

shouted for help, for Rose, for the hands of time to turn back and undo the tragedy that had befallen my best friend, but nothing happened. Then, I slipped into darkness.

My SHEETS and nightgown were soaked through with sweat. I wiped my hand across my forehead and then placed it in my lap, looking at the way my hand tapered down to my wrist. At the way the delicate bones ran from my wrist up to my elbow and to my shoulder. I'd never thought to be grateful for the everyday mechanics of my body, but in that moment, I was so relieved to find my hand firmly attached to the rest of me.

I'd had to wash my sheets too many times to count since moving into my new London home. Something about living alone had brought the nightmares of the Simla explosion back to the forefront of my mind. They were more vivid, more enduring. On the ship from Bombay to London and at Ashton House, I'd been able to rouse myself from the dreams, but now I had to live the entire experience over again before my subconscious mind would release me. I woke several times a week in a pool of my own sweat, heart pounding in my ears, eyes wide and searching for a glimpse of the man who had ended the lives of the people I'd called family for the better part of ten years.

I kicked my blankets down to the end of the bed and swung my feet over the side. If the last few nights were to be any judge, sleep would be elusive now that I'd woken up. I tried to step carefully across the wooden floor. Aseem slept in the servant's quarters, which were located just below my bedroom, and my sleeplessness had begun to worry him.

It felt strange to be worried about by a twelve-year-old, but I'd known since the moment I'd seen him aboard the *RMS Star of India* that he was wise beyond his years. And most importantly, Aseem was loyal. He made an incredibly useful errand boy and he asked few questions, which, in my opinion, was one of his best qualities. Still, if he heard me walking around in the middle of the night, he would mention it over breakfast and insist I take an afternoon nap.

I tip-toed to the curtains and pulled them back, letting in the moonlight. I'd assumed it was still the middle of the night, so I was surprised to see the beginnings of color leaching over the horizon. The sun would rise within the next hour, meaning I'd slept longer than I had all week.

I loved the view from my bedroom window, and found myself standing there, enjoying it frequently. Never in my life would I have thought I'd have my own house, especially not one so nice. But ever since I'd shed my old identity and stepped into the life of my dearly departed friend Rose Beckingham, doors I'd never even known existed were opening to me. With her inheritance, even though I had to collect it in monthly installments, I had a level of independence I'd never dreamed of. And more than that, I had the means to finally solve the mystery that had been plaguing me since I first left New York as a child: what had happened to my missing brother?

Something on the street below my window caught my attention, and I squinted down into the early morning darkness. A figure, a man in a long coat and a hat, lurked beneath a streetlight, standing just at the edge of the circle of light so his face was hidden in shadow. His shoulders were squared with my window, and based on the angle of his neck, I could tell he was looking up at me.

Startled, I stepped away from the window and back into the privacy of my room. I squeezed my eyes closed. Perhaps I was still dreaming. I shook my head and then resumed my position at the window. I glanced down hesitantly, and the man was still there. My pulse quickened.

Before I could do anything other than stare down at him in confusion and growing fear, he bowed slightly at the hips, tipped his hat at me, and walked away down the sidewalk. I watched him disappear when he turned at the end of the block.

As soon as he was gone, the terror that had gripped me at the sight of him began to fade, replaced with a flurry of questions. Who was the man? What did he want? What would he have done had I not chosen that moment to go to my window?

A chill ran through me. I didn't know the man's true intentions, but I knew enough to feel threatened. He had tipped his hat to me before leaving. He wanted me to know that he knew I'd seen him, and he wanted me to realize that he didn't care.

I pulled the curtains closed and moved to sit on the edge of my bed. Even if I'd still been tired, it would have been impossible for me to fall asleep. Between the nightmares and the mysterious man, my brain was operating at full speed. I just didn't want to move downstairs and begin the day so early because it would force the rest of the house to wake up, as well. Though I told Aseem and George, my driver, I was more than capable of doing things on my own, they each woke up as soon as I did, which meant we'd all been getting a rather early start since moving into the new house.

I sat on the edge of my bed long enough that I had almost convinced myself the man at my window had been a continuation of my nightmare. I'd been in the flux space between dreaming and waking, and the man had been nothing more than a figment.

When I finally went down for breakfast, however, and Aseem handed me an unmarked box that had been left on the sidewalk outside, I knew the man had been all too real.

"You didn't see who left it?" I asked, taking the box from his hands and setting it on the dining room table.

Aseem shook his head, his dark brown eyes wide and honest. "No, Miss Rose. I went outside this morning and it was sitting in the middle of the sidewalk."

I studied the box without touching it. Though I had seen Aseem carry it in rather roughly, part of me still felt as though it would explode at the slightest touch. Though, perhaps that had more to do with what had transpired in India than any real cause for concern.

"Were you expecting something?" he asked.

"No, I wasn't, but thank you for bring this to me." I nodded my head and Aseem, astute for his young age, took that as his cue to leave. He carefully pulled the dining room doors closed behind him, leaving me alone with the box.

I studied the package for a few more seconds. It appeared to be innocuous. Medium-sized, roughly the size of a dinner plate, and wrapped in plain brown paper, it could have come from anywhere and been meant for anyone. Yet, somehow, I knew it was intended for me. The man standing outside my window had meant for me to see him lurking there. He meant for me to find this package. Despite an overwhelming urge to throw the box into the fire and go about my day as though the entire incident had never happened, I knew I wouldn't be able to rest until I knew what secrets the box contained. So, steeling myself, I moved forward, slipping my finger beneath the careful wrapping, and tore it open.

Sitting in the perfect center of the box was a chess piece. A pawn, to be exact. I had never been any good at chess and I'd played very infrequently, but still I recognized the piece. Beneath the pawn was a thick card folded in half. Without touching the pawn, I grabbed the card and slipped it from the bottom of the box. Unfolding it, I began to read.

Miss Dennet,

I hope you will not mind my use of your previous name. I do not fancy pretenses, and calling you Rose Beckingham would be a pretense of the falsest kind. As my greeting has no doubt made you aware, I am familiar with your story. Your investigation into the recent murder of Frederick Grossmith brought you to my attention. I was impressed with your handling of the case and sought to understand why an heiress would busy herself with the death of a man of no importance. The answer to that question lead me to the truth that you are not an heiress, but a pretender.

If you find yourself frightened at my knowing your secret, I urge you to be calm. I do not intend to share my knowledge with anyone. In fact, I wish to share some knowledge with you. If you are able to earn it.

In my research into you and your purpose here in London, I learned of your search for your long-lost brother, Jimmy. I hold a key piece of the puzzle that could lead you to Jimmy. The piece is yours should you choose to put your detective skills to work and solve a crime for me.

A PERSON WILL BE MURDERED *this weekend in Somerset. If you can apprehend the killer after the crime has been committed, the information I have will be yours.*

I EAGERLY AWAIT YOUR DECISION.

2

"And you did not see the person's face?" Achilles Prideaux asked, pouring me a cup of tea.

I shook my head. "No, I only saw a shadowy figure and then I awoke to the mysterious package."

"And there was nothing distinctive about the package?"

I thought back on it, trying to recall any other details, but there was nothing. "Nothing aside from ordinary wrapping paper. It was not even addressed."

"How do you know it was meant for you, then?" Achilles asked.

"Because of the letter inside." I did not tell Monsieur Prideaux that the letter was addressed to my true identity, Nellie Dennet, and not to Rose Beckingham, but that hardly mattered. In either case, I was the intended recipient.

Achilles sat down in the chair across from me and folded his hands on the table in front of him. "Tell me everything again."

I'd tried to keep the mysterious package to myself, not wanting to worry anyone in my household with its contents, but it had proven to be impossible. Whoever had sent it knew my true identity, and they forewarned me of a murder. Wasn't it my duty, then, to report it? I wanted to take the matter to the police, but I could not do that without showing them the letter. And I could not show anyone the letter without revealing my secret and announcing to the world that I was not Rose Beckingham. So, I'd gone to Achilles Prideaux. Although he was a detective, he was a private detective, which meant I was not required to show or tell him anything I did not wish to. This fact had been proven when Achilles agreed to help me search for my brother, Jimmy, despite the fact I had withheld from him that Jimmy was my brother. As far as Monsieur Prideaux knew, I had hired him to track down an old friend who had disappeared.

So, I'd left home just after breakfast and arrived at Achilles' house less than ten minutes later. I'd had no idea at the time I purchased my house how convenient it would be to live so close to a detective.

I repeated the story. I walked Monsieur Prideaux through waking from my nightmare, the shadowy figure below my window, the package Aseem found, and the letter and pawn inside. I left out all incriminating details that pointed to my true identity, and I had intentionally left the box and its contents at home, lest their examination by the detective reveal more of my own secrets than I wished him to guess.

When I finished, he leaned back in his chair and stared at the ceiling for so long I wondered whether he'd forgotten I was sitting across from him. I could tell Achilles was tired. He had just returned from a quick trip related to his detective work. His already tan skin looked to be a richer brown after days spent in the sun. He certainly stood out amongst the pale color palette of London. Light-skinned people, gray skies, pale stones. Though, Achilles didn't need any help standing out. His thin mustache gave him an air of mystery and the cane he carried, which I knew to hide a thin blade in the bottom, was an eye-catcher. He really was a handsome man. Except for that mustache. I would have shaved the mustache myself if I thought I could have done it before he'd realize.

"Well," I finally said, interrupting his thoughts. "What do you think I should do about the murder the sender mentioned?"

His mouth twisted to the side, the mustache twisting with it. "Nothing," he said firmly.

"Nothing?" I asked. "We have been warned about a possible murder and you want to do nothing about it?"

He shook his head. "I want *you* to do nothing about it. I want to investigate the sender of this message and see what information can be found."

"We have no clues with which to begin a search," I said. "We have no reason to believe any information can be found. Am I really supposed to sit by while an innocent person is murdered?"

"First, I have ways of finding things out," Achilles said, winking at me. "It is my job to solve the impossible. Second, we do not know the intended victim is innocent. You make too many assumptions, Mademoiselle, and I worry they will put you in danger."

"My life is not the one that was threatened," I reminded him. I did not like feeling as though I needed protecting. I'd found my way out of more than my fair share of life or death scrapes. Though, now that I was thinking about it, Achilles had helped me escape the first scrape and my cousin Edward had helped me escape the second. I shook my head, pushing the thought aside so I could focus on the matter at hand.

"This message could be a prank. If it is, there is no need to worry yourself about it or alarm the public. If it is not a prank, however," Achilles said, holding one finger in the air, "Then the person who sent you the package is obviously a criminal or has criminal ties. I know of no other way in which someone can be aware of an impending murder. In which case, accepting the challenge will only put you in danger."

"So, whether the person is a criminal or not, you do not want me to involve myself?" I asked for clarification.

"It is dangerous, Rose. I know you have had brushes with danger and murderers in the past and come away unharmed, but at some point, your luck will run out. And I, for one, do not wish to see any harm befall you."

I took a sip of my tea and returned the cup to the saucer. "Are you saying you are fond of me, Monsieur Prideaux?" I asked, raising an eyebrow and looking up at him.

Achilles looked suddenly nervous. He fidgeted in his seat, shifting from side to side, and then ran a finger along the length of his mustache. "It is my job to solve crimes. Should you die, I would no doubt be called upon to find your killer, and I have enough work to keep me busy as it is."

I grabbed my cream sweater from the back of the chair and slipped it on over my mauve buttoned blouse. "If I do find myself murdered, I'll do my best to schedule it for when your calendar isn't so full," I teased.

Achilles stood up and walked me towards his front door. "I certainly appreciate that, Mademoiselle Rose. Though, you should know that finding your murderer would be my top priority regardless of my schedule."

I was already on the steps, but I turned back to see him

smiling at me. I wondered for the briefest of seconds whether this hadn't been the detective's attempt at flirting, but then he quickly warned me not to do anything with the information in the letter and slammed the door, killing the thought.

3

W hen I'd moved out of Lord and Lady Ashton's home the week before, I wondered whether they would truly miss me as much as they claimed they would. I'd only lived with them a few weeks before finding my own place, and before that, I hadn't seen them for over ten years. We weren't a normal family, and somewhere in the back of my mind, I assumed we would drift apart. Those fears were quelled, though, by Lady Ashton's constant dinner invitations. In the seven days I'd been gone, she'd invited me every single night.

"She is a young woman with her own home," Lord Ashton had said the third time I accepted Lady Ashton's dinner invitation. "Certainly Rose has better ways she'd enjoy spending her time."

"Rose likes seeing us," Alice argued, taking her father's word as a personal affront.

"Of course, I do." I smiled at my youngest cousin.

Alice was fifteen, eight years younger than me, but she and I were by far the closest of all of my cousins. Catherine and I had made moves towards being friendlier, but we were still a long way from being anywhere close to friends. And Edward, the eldest, had proven the most difficult Beckingham to form a connection with. Even after the events of the preceding weeks when he had saved me from being shot and killed by the murderer of Frederick Grossmith, Edward seemed distant. I'd always heard that the strongest friendships were forged in fire, but apparently gunfire was immune.

"And I really appreciate the delicious dinners," I continued. "They are much more lavish than I could ever cook for myself."

"Rose, dear," Lady Ashton said, placing a hand on her chest. "You must hire yourself a cook."

"I'm still working on filling out my home's staff," I said, deciding not to tell Lady Ashton I wasn't certain I could afford a cook. I had Rose's inheritance, but until I found a husband, I could only receive it in monthly payments. The stipulation in my father's will felt beyond antiquated, but there was nothing I could do about it except make the best of the situation.

"Good for you for taking your time," Lord Ashton said. "It is important to be able to trust those who help run your household."

I sensed a bit of a warning in my uncle's words. He and Lady Ashton were less than thrilled when I decided to hire George as my driver only a few hours after they fired him. It was true I had briefly thought George might be Frederick Grossmith's murderer, but I had realized my mistake and had no further reason to doubt his loyalty. My aunt and uncle, however, did not appreciate the discovery that George had lied to them about his criminal past. His misdeeds were minor and nowhere close to murder, but they still dismissed him, and I decided his ability to keep a secret made him an asset to me.

"Yes, absolutely, Uncle," I said, smiling.

After my sleepless night and my meeting with Achilles Prideaux, I had wanted nothing more than to go home and enjoy the solitude of my own house. However, Lady Ashton sent a servant to deliver an invitation to dinner. She expressed several times in the short letter that she had something of the highest importance to discuss with me. So, when I sat down at the dinner table with my family, I expected the discussion to revolve around my inheritance or a death in the family. I was bracing myself for an upheaval of some kind, news that would throw my life out of orbit.

"Rose," Lady Ashton began, adjusting a lace napkin in her lap and smiling across the table at me, her lips pursed. "We would all love nothing more than for you to join us this weekend at our family's country estate."

I blinked several times and glanced around the table. Everyone, save Edward and Lord Ashton, was looking at me with wide smiles stretched across their faces. Alice seemed close to bouncing right out of her seat with excitement.

Was this the important topic my aunt had wanted to discuss? Surely not. A weekend getaway wasn't something that had to be discussed over dinner. Lady Ashton could have simply telephoned me or written the request in her invitation.

"Well," I began, trying to work out how to excuse myself from going without seeming rude. "Things at my house are still in a bit of disarray. It would be pretty difficult to leave so soon after moving in."

Lady Ashton's smile fell. She stared at me in thinly veiled horror, as if I'd just announced to everyone that I enjoyed killing stray cats.

"You aren't going to come with us?" Alice asked, eyes wide and glassy. Was she about to cry?

"I'm just not sure if it would be a good idea right now," I said.

Lady Ashton cleared her throat and straightened up in her seat. "I'm sure we can all understand your predicament," she said in a way that was not at all understanding.

I nodded and started in on the first course, trying to ignore the heavy silence surrounding me. I kept waiting for Lady Ashton to move on to the very important topic she had mentioned in her letter, but she didn't seem in any sort of hurry to begin a new conversation, and I had to wonder whether the weekend trip to the family estate hadn't been the urgent matter she needed to discuss with me. Finally, when the silence became too much to bear, I laid my silverware down on the table and cleared my throat, drawing my aunt's reluctant attention.

"Is there anything else you needed to discuss with me, Aunt?" I asked as delicately as I could.

She looked confused and then shook her head. "No, I do not believe so."

"Oh." So, the weekend getaway had been the important matter at hand. That would be good to know for future. The Beckinghams took their holiday plans very seriously. On any other weekend, I would have accepted the offer. After receiving the mysterious letter that morning, however, I felt like my attention was being pulled towards that. Achilles Prideaux had told me not to get involved, but how could I not? The author of the letter claimed to have information about Jimmy, and since they seemed to know all of my secrets, I had no reason to doubt them. In truth, it would be nice to have my family out of the city for the weekend, so I could focus on the puzzle without being distracted.

"Rose!" Alice practically shouted, dropping her napkin in her lap.

"Alice," Lord Ashton warned, his voice deep and booming. "There is no need for such hysterics."

It was astounding to me that Lord Ashton was Alice's father, yet could still be surprised by her frequent and passionate outbursts.

Alice continued without hesitation. "You have to come with us this weekend. I will be bored silly in the country without you there to keep me company."

"Rose cannot help it if she is busy," Catherine said, patting the back of her younger sister's hand and smiling an apology at me. "She can come to Somerset with us next time."

Suddenly, my interest was piqued. "Somerset?"

Catherine and Alice both nodded at once.

"The family estate is in Somerset?" I asked, hoping for more of an answer this time.

"Didn't you know that?" Lady Ashton asked. "I thought you and your parents had been to the estate before."

I'd become so comfortable with the Beckinghams that occasionally I forgot I was only impersonating their niece. The real Rose Beckingham had an entire life with these people before I knew her. She had probably spent countless weekends at the family estate with her own parents, romping around the countryside with her cousins.

"Of course, I have been," I said, shaking my head and smiling. "I just forgot it was in Somerset."

"It's beautiful up there," Alice said, still trying to sell me on the family trip.

"I thought you just said you'd be bored silly there without Rose," Edward said, speaking up for the first time since I'd arrived.

Alice shot him a dirty look. "Just because I find the country boring doesn't mean it isn't beautiful."

Edward said something sly back to his sister, but I didn't hear it. My mind was busy mentally rereading the mysterious letter from that morning. The author had warned me that a murder would occur this weekend in Somerset. Could it be a coincidence? I didn't know my family was heading to the countryside until this very minute, but could the author have somehow known in advance?

The chess piece stuck out in my mind. I hadn't paid much attention to it when I'd first opened the box, but now I wondered whether it wasn't a hint at the type of game the mysterious writer liked to play. The writer was a chess master with a view of the entire gameboard, whereas I only had a single, spent pawn. If I wanted any chance at learning the Chess Master's identity, I needed to sneak a peek at the board. And I had a suspicion that could only happen in Somerset.

"Don't listen to him, Rose," Alice said, waving away whatever Edward had just said. "Like I said, with the right company, the family estate can be a wonderful time."

Catherine nodded her head. "I have to agree. The company is everything."

Edward rolled his eyes at both of his sisters and returned his attention to his plate, mumbling something about the countryside feeling crowded.

Could these people, who I had mostly come to love and cherish, be in danger? Was the Chess Master, as I had begun to think of him, threatening my family with his ominous note? By the way Lady Ashton had treated the subject with such reverence, I knew there was no hope of convincing them to stay in London for the weekend. And I couldn't show them the letter without opening the lid on a lot of issues I would rather keep to myself. So, if my family would be going to the Somerset countryside completely unaware of the possible dangers that awaited them, it was my responsibility to tag along and try to keep them safe. Achilles Prideaux had warned me not to get involved, but it seemed as if the Chess Master was making that impossible.

"You've all convinced me," I said suddenly, causing all other table conversation to cease.

Lady Ashton gasped. Alice once again began to bounce up and down with excitement. Catherine smiled. Even Lord Ashton winked at me across the long table. Edward seemed to be the only person who offered up no reaction, aside from a scowl and violently stabbing his fork into the meat on his plate.

I knew I couldn't let the Beckinghams stumble into a dangerous situation without trying to assist them. But as much as I wanted to pretend my motives were pure, I also knew I couldn't pass up the opportunity to receive information about my brother Jimmy. Based on what the Chess Master had written in his note, a murder would occur in Somerset whether I was in attendance or not, so it figured I should go and give myself a chance at solving the crime

Lady Ashton clapped her hands, redirecting my attention. "This weekend is going to be so much fun."

4

——————

Although Aseem had found the mysterious box outside of my house, I hadn't revealed the contents to him or explained why I'd rushed to meet with Achilles Prideaux right after opening it. But still, I got the impression he sensed something was slightly amiss about my weekend plans with the Beckinghams.

"Are you certain you ought to travel this weekend?" he asked for the third time as he placed my luggage out on the sidewalk for George to load into the car.

"It will only be for a couple of days, Aseem," I said, trying to reassure him.

The young boy nodded. "I could come and assist you with anything you might need while you are there."

"You would be much more useful to me here," I said. "There is so much unpacking still left to do. And I would enjoy my time away more knowing my home will be in capable hands."

George coughed behind me, and I turned to smile at him. "In two sets of capable hands," I amended.

Though George was obviously grateful to me for hiring

him after the Beckinghams let him go, he didn't take particularly kindly to being made equals with a twelve-year-old. I knew he would see how mature Aseem was over time, but until then, he would need reassurance.

Aseem waved reluctantly from the corner as George maneuvered the car into the traffic and headed for the train station. He dropped me off at the end of the block at my urging.

"I can take you to the front entrance," George said.

"No, it's fine, George. I don't want you to have to face the entire Beckingham family so soon after your dismissal."

He laughed. "I can assure you it will not bother me in the slightest. Their opinion of me is no longer important. The only thing that matters is that I am a quality driver to you, and I would not be a quality driver if I didn't deliver you directly to your destination."

"I appreciate your loyalty, but you would not be a quality driver if you disregarded my wishes. Lord and Lady Ashton didn't want me to hire you, so I do not wish to flaunt my decision to do so. Dropping me at the end of the block is as much for my sake as it is yours."

In the end, George relented, and I carried my own luggage to the train.

Edward raised an eyebrow as I approached and reached for my luggage.

"Thank you," I said, allowing him to help me. Normally, I would have insisted I could do it myself, but I was still desperate to make a connection with Edward and refusing his help didn't seem like a good way to do that. As he finished with my luggage, he turned back to me. "Is your driver injured? Typically, he would deliver your bags to the train."

Edward spoke of George as though he did not know him

and the cool look in his eyes let me know his offer of assistance had been little more than a reason to criticize my decision to hire George. I'd confided George's past to Edward and asked him not to tell his parents. I swore to him that George was a good man, that his past no longer defined him, but Edward immediately shared the information and George had lost his job. Now, Edward wanted to try and prove to me that he had been correct in his decision and that I shouldn't have hired the chauffer.

"George wanted to see me safely on the train, but I insisted he stay with the car and avoid the foot traffic. Anyway, what are cousins for, after all?" I tried to keep my tone light and playful, but I knew Edward and I were in a sparring match. Each conversation determined who had the upper hand, and I didn't want to let Edward thing he had any kind of power over me.

"Rose!" Alice ran up and wrapped her arms around my waist. Even though she was as excitable as ever, even in the short time since I'd arrived in London, I could see that Alice was growing from a girl into a woman. "I'm so glad you decided to come. This weekend will be much more enjoyable now that you are here."

"That's sweet of you to say." I wrapped my arms around her shoulders and squeezed, grateful at least one of my cousins liked me.

"We had better take our seats," Catherine said, ushering Alice and I onto the train, where we joined Lord and Lady Ashton who were sitting in a quiet back corner of one of the train cars. They had an entire bench and a two-person seat waiting.

"I was beginning to wonder whether you'd changed your mind," Lady Ashton said, waving for me to take the seat next to her. I accepted it and Alice squeezed in next to me. Catherine and Edward took the double seat.

"Of course, I didn't," I said, thinking of the Chess Master's message. *A person will be murdered this weekend in Somerset.*

"I'm really looking forward to this weekend," I forced myself to say with a smile.

"We are going to introduce you to everyone," Catherine said, leaning over the back of her seat to join the conversation. "Reintroduce you, that is."

"You will have met most everyone who will be there," Lady Ashton said. "They have been neighbors of the estate and friends of the family for as long as we've owned it, but a lot of time has passed since you were last there and you are no longer a child."

"Yes, I will definitely need to refresh my memory," I said, relieved that no one would expect me to remember any names or faces. Even if I had been the real Rose Beckingham, remembering the details of adults I hadn't seen since I was a young teenager would be difficult, but considering I had never really met any of them before, it would have been completely impossible.

"There will be plenty of time for that. Everyone will be staying with us at Ridgewick Hall for the entire weekend, and I have a small surprise for you, Rose," Lady Ashton said.

"A surprise for me?"

She nodded excitedly and then stared at me, eyebrows raised.

"What is the surprise?" I finally asked, realizing she wasn't going to give the information unprompted.

Lady Ashton clasped her hands together in front of her and smiled. "I invited Mr. and Mrs. Worthing to join us for the weekend."

"Oh," I said, blankly. I didn't know what kind of surprise I'd expected, but it wasn't that. "How did you come into contact with them?" The Worthings were definitely in a lower social station than the Beckinghams and under normal circumstances, wouldn't have been invited to spend a weekend on their family estate. In fact, I found it surprising Lady Ashton had even thought of them.

"We stayed in touch after they reached out to inform us they would be travelling to London with you on the ship. They are such lovely people," she said.

The Worthings had been family friends of Rose's parents while they lived in India. Mr. Worthing had retired and was planning to come back to London at the same time the explosion happened. They were the people who wrongly identified me as Rose Beckingham while I was recovering in the hospital. Then, they stepped in and acted as my chaperones aboard the *RMS Star of India*. While I found them to be very kind people, I also didn't understand how spending a weekend with them was a special surprise.

"I thought it might be nice for you to have someone there this weekend who you knew well. I wanted to contact some of your friends, but I've never heard you mention anyone specifically and no one had ever come by the house to see you."

Edward was half-turned towards us, so he could hear the conversation, and I could see his mouth pulling into a smile. No doubt he was enjoying Lady Ashton's description of me as unsocial and practically friendless.

"That was very kind of you, Aunt," I said, cutting her off. "It will be wonderful to see them again."

Lady Ashton turned to her husband and Edward turned back to Catherine, both groups talking amongst themselves, while Alice began telling me everything she hoped to show me over the weekend. I couldn't focus on her words, though. Mr. and Mrs. Worthing would be there this weekend. I'd decided to come to the family estate out of concern for my family members, but now I had to look out for the Worthings, as well. And worst of all, they were invited to the event purely for my benefit. Had it not been for their connection to me, they would have remained safely in London.

I had to wonder whether the Chess Master knew Lady Ashton would invite the Worthings or whether they would be a surprise to him, as well. And then, for the first time, I wondered whether the Chess Master already knew who would die. The letter had made it clear there would be a murder, but there was no indication that a victim had already been selected. Was anyone safe?

After a few minutes, Alice let the steady rumble of the train lull her to sleep, her head resting on my shoulder, and I used the quiet to think about how I would keep everyone I cared about safe over the weekend.

The Chess Master had indicated that my task was not to stop the murder from happening, but to solve the crime. I looked from the sleeping Alice to Catherine and Edward, and then to their parents, Lady and Lord Ashton, and felt the weight of responsibility crushing down on me. I didn't know if I'd be able to save any of them, but I knew I had to try.

5

A car and chauffer were waiting for us when we got off the train, and by the time we made the long drive to Ridgewick, everyone was travel weary and ready to stretch.

The car drove up a long gravel drive and stopped in front of a wide, shallow set of stairs that lead to the front doors of the house. Everyone piled out of the car while the driver unloaded the luggage. As a servant in a dark uniform came out to assist the chauffer, I found myself staring up at the house, taking in the grandeur of it all.

"Is it just like you remember?" Lady Ashton asked, standing next to me and flattening the wrinkles from the skirt of her dress and adjusting her scalloped-brim hat.

"It looks entirely different. Almost as if I've never been here," I said, smiling.

My aunt patted my back. "One quick tour around the property and you'll remember your way around well enough. Do not fret."

Several more servants came down to greet the Beckinghams and carry our bags inside and the men followed them to supervise just as another car pulled up the drive and stopped behind ours. Mrs. Worthing's face was pressed up against the glass, her eyes wide as they took in the house.

I could imagine exactly how Mrs. Worthing must have felt on seeing Ridgewick Hall for the first time. Especially since I had just seen it for the first time myself.

The stone building was three stories tall with columns that ran the entire face of the house from top to bottom, forming a covered portico. The matching stone pediment atop the columns was decorated with intricately carved flowers and vines. The same details had been added around the windows that dotted the front façade at regular intervals. The structure was both imposing and delicate, matching the landscaping that surrounded it. The nearest trees were hulking and ancient, but sunlight shone through the lacework of leaves and branches, painting everything in dappled gold. It really was a beautiful property.

The car door opened and Mrs. Worthing scrambled out, followed by her husband. It was clear by the tangle of pearls around her neck and the large flower that decorated her silk hat that Mrs. Worthing was dressed to impress. She was aware of the Beckingham's social status and wanted to look the part of a respectable guest. Mr. Worthing looked mostly unchanged except for the sparkling silver cuff links at his wrists.

"Rose, my dear," Mrs. Worthing called, placing her gloved hands over her mouth as though she could burst into tears at the sight of me. "I am so glad to see you again."

She wrapped me in a hug and, consequently, in the strong floral scent of her perfume.

"I'm glad to see you, as well," I said, hugging her back and nodding at Mr. Worthing over her shoulder.

Mr. Worthing smiled and then tipped his head to all of

the ladies. "I suppose I should take our luggage up to the house and give my greetings to the gentlemen."

"Oh no, Mr. Worthing," Lady Ashton said. "I wouldn't hear of it. Leave your bags here and a servant will come collect them. Do feel free, however, to move on up to the main house."

Mr. Worthing raised his eyebrows at his wife, clearly impressed that he wouldn't have to carry his own belongings, and turned towards the house.

"How have you been since I've seen you last, dear girl?" Mrs. Worthing asked, wrapping her arm around mine and moving towards the stairs.

I told her about how kind the Beckinghams had been and about finding my own house, but conveniently left out the part about investigating another murder and nearly being killed yet again.

"How have you and Mr. Worthing been?" I asked. "Do you enjoy London as much as you did India?"

Mrs. Worthing used her free hand to tangle her fingers in her pearls and rolled her eyes. "My dear, I much prefer London to India. It is so much cooler. Not to mention, now that Mr. Worthing is retired, we have all the time in the world to enjoy what the city has to offer. In Bombay, he was always working. He'd get to the office early, stay at the office late, and come home long enough to eat and sleep before starting all over again. Now, we are able to have a social life, and I adore it."

"That is lovely," I said. "It sounds like retirement suits you both just fine."

"Indeed," she said. "I was so pleased to receive an invitation from Lady Ashton to join you this weekend. It was quite the surprise."

"For me, as well," I said. "My aunt wanted me to be with

friends this weekend and she thought of you and Mr. Worthing."

This sounded much more flattering than the truth, which was that I had no other friends and my aunt could think of no one else to invite.

Mrs. Worthing placed a hand over her heart and pulled her lips back in a tight smile. "Well, we are beyond flattered that you count us as friends and that the good lady thought of us. We are looking forward to a very exciting weekend."

Once again, the Chess Master came to my mind. Was everyone around me in incredible danger? Would I be able to save those I cared about? As Mrs. Worthing and I moved to the steps to wait for the rest of the guests to arrive, I made a vow to keep my eyes open and stay vigilant.

THE REST of the Beckingham's guests arrived within the hour. The first to arrive was Lady Harwood and her personal physician, Dr. Shaw. The old woman lived on a property only a short distance away, but according to Lady Ashton's hurried whisper as her car arrived, she rarely left her home for fear of catching some illness.

"She is constantly convinced she is coming down with tuberculosis and the plague. She can't walk up a flight of stairs without fear of breaking a bone or dislocating a joint. The woman is a strain on my nerves, but I couldn't invite the other neighbors without also extending an invitation to her," Lady Ashton said.

"Well, of course not," Mrs. Worthing agreed. "You had to do your neighborly duty."

"I didn't think for a minute she would agree to come, but she surprised me."

Just then, the old woman managed to climb up the stairs with the assistance of Dr. Shaw, complaining the entire way, and stood before us, panting and moaning.

"Everyone insists on stairs," she said, shaking her head. "I had the stairs in front of my house removed so my driver could deliver me directly to the front door. Perhaps you should consider the same thing, Lady Ashton."

"Perhaps I should, Lady Harwood. Thank you again for joining us this weekend," my aunt said, touching the old woman's hand lightly. "And Dr. Shaw, we are pleased to have you, as well."

The doctor, a middle-aged man with sloping shoulders and a soft chin smiled and nodded but said nothing in return. It seemed as if he was either a quiet man by nature or Lady Harwood's constant complaining had sucked away his desire for conversation.

Next came Mr. and Miss Barry. They were a young couple who appeared to be around my age, both incredibly blonde. It looked as though their hair was made from actual sunlight.

"What are the chances of a couple both having hair that vibrant shade of yellow?" I remarked.

Lady Ashton put a single finger over her lips and smiled. "Don't let them hear you say that. Charles and Vivian are brother and sister, and they are very sensitive about that subject. Most people mistake them for a couple."

"Oh, I'm sorry," I said, cheeks flushing. This was something the real Rose Beckingham would have known. "I made a hasty assumption."

"And once you spend time with them, you'll realize it was an easy assumption to make. They behave more like a husband and wife than a brother and sister, but do not let them hear you say so."

Mrs. Worthing simply clacked her tongue and watched as Charles unloaded Vivian's suitcase and then took her hand to assist her up the stairs.

"My sister and I are pleased to join you for the weekend," Charles said once Lady Ashton had made all the introductions.

Vivian nodded. "Yes, my brother and I have been looking forward to it all week."

I wondered whether they would begin every sentence by announcing their relationship to one another and made a mental note to keep track of it over the course of the weekend.

"I believe I see Catherine and her brother up near the house," Charles said, quickly reclaiming his sister's hand as they moved towards the house.

Last to arrive was the most surprising guest. Even more surprising than the Worthings. Mr. Matcham looked like a man better suited for a gambling establishment on a bad side of the city than an estate in the countryside. Everything about him was sleek. His hair, his dark suit, his voice.

"Hello, esteemed hostess," he said, bowing to Lady Ashton in a way that looked respectful, but felt like an exaggeration. "I'm looking forward to our weekend together."

Lady Ashton's mouth tightened into a straight line. "Yes, we are all excited for good weather and friendly company."

I sensed a hint of a warning in Lady Ashton's words, and I must not have been alone in that because Mrs. Worthing bit her lower lip nervously and began to fidget.

Mr. Matcham smiled up at us a moment too long, his teeth glinting in the sunlight before he looked past us and waved. I turned to see Catherine walking down the path, Edward close behind.

"If you'll excuse me," Mr. Matcham said, bowing to us

and moving towards my cousins. He met Catherine with a nod followed by a hug. Then, a firm handshake for Edward.

Lady Ashton let out a long sigh and then shook her head as though shaking away a cobweb. "Well, Mr. Matcham was the last guest to arrive. Everyone is here and the festivities can officially begin. Would you care to walk with me, Mrs. Worthing?" Lady Ashton extended her elbow to the other woman, who took it eagerly, and they walked towards the house.

I turned and watched the homeowners and guests mingling across the property. Lord Ashton was pointing up at the house, directing Mr. Worthing's attention to some fine detail in the architecture. Catherine and Edward were splitting their attention between Charles and Vivian Barry and Mr. Matcham. Lady Ashton and Mrs. Worthing were giggling like old friends. And Alice was waving desperately for me to join her under the shade of a large tree. I took note of each person, and wondered which of them, if any, would be the victim the Chess Master had promised. Then, I looked at them again, this time wondering who the culprit could be.

"Rose," Alice called, breaking into my thoughts. "Come over here."

I smiled at my youngest cousin and prayed silently for her safety. "Coming, Alice. You impatient girl."

6

Once everyone was gathered in the front of the house, Lady Ashton insisted the day was too lovely to spend indoors.

"A walking tour would be lovely, don't you think, Lord Ashton?" she asked, not leaving room for her husband to disagree.

So, the unconventional party, save for Lady Harwood who retired immediately to the Hall and only barely allowed Dr. Shaw to leave her side long enough to view the property, was off. I took up the rear, glad for the opportunity to observe all of the guests together. Once everyone was inside the house, they would be in the dining room, in the library, in their individual bedrooms. Everyone would find their respective places within the home and stay there, mingling only with those they wished to mingle with. The walk was one of the few times, aside from meals, where everyone would be together, and I could talk privately with them all.

I wanted to believe the Beckinghams retiring to Ridgewick Hall for the weekend was a coincidence, but clearly the Chess Master knew of their plans before I did. So, assuming my theory was correct and the note and the chess piece and the murder were not some elaborate prank, one of the guests visiting Ridgewick Hall was contemplating a murder. Which meant I had to try and thwart the killer. The letter implied that would be impossible, but it felt wrong not to try. Of course, somewhere in the back of my mind I knew that if the murder didn't occur, then there would be nothing to solve and I would not receive my promised reward, information about my brother Jimmy.

Not for the first time, I wished for the counsel of Achilles Prideaux. Of course, he had already advised me not to become involved with the case, but that was before either of us knew my family would be in Somerset that weekend. I could have telephoned or had Aseem deliver a note to Achilles, explaining my whereabouts and plans, but I didn't think it would be a good idea. Knowing Monsieur Prideaux and his talent for showing up unexpectedly, he would have appeared suddenly at Ridgewick, and I did not want to have to explain to Lord and Lady Ashton why their niece was keeping such close company with a private detective.

Lord and Lady Ashton took the lead, remarking on notable landmarks and estates in the distance. Dr. Shaw was the only guest who showed even the slightest interest in their commentary. Everyone else lagged behind so as to talk more freely. Charles and Vivian Barry walked just in front of me, linked arm in arm.

"Some of this brush ought to be cleared away," Vivian said, kicking at a tree root with the toe of her heels.

"Now, now, sister," Charles said, squeezing his sister's arm playfully. "Some people enjoy a rugged walk through nature. That is why people come to the countryside, after all."

"I come for the quiet, not for the shrubbery," Vivian responded. Edward was walking just in front of Vivian, and she leaned forward, placing her free hand on Edward's shoulder. "Don't you agree, Edward?"

"Yes, I quite enjoy the quiet," Edward responded, placing a special emphasis on the word 'quiet.'

Vivian didn't seem to notice this. She giggled loudly, making me jump, and unwound herself from her brother to move up next to Edward, taking Catherine's place. She wore a cream chiffon tea dress that floated delicately around her calves and her shoulders were wrapped in a lacelike knitted matching sweater that fell well below her hips. With every step along the muddy path, I worried mud would kick up onto her light-colored outfit.

Catherine shifted back as Vivian elbowed her way closer to Edward, falling into step with Charles, who did not seem at all displeased by the shift in walking partners. He studied Catherine's profile in earnest before picking up the conversation again. "I, myself, come to the countryside for the company," he said with a wink.

Catherine nodded at him politely, her lips pulling back into the barest definition of a smile. "Yes, we have a good group this weekend."

It was clear from where I was standing that the Barry siblings had found themselves rather taken with the respective Beckingham siblings. However, the Ashton siblings did not seem to reciprocate these feelings. Even though Vivian's arm was wound around Edward's elbow, he was holding it as far away from his side as possible, as though he would prefer to detach it from his body altogether rather than risk accidentally brushing against Vivian's skin. And Charles couldn't take his eyes away from Catherine, but she had her sights set further up the trail and paid him little to no mind.

"I'm so pleased Rose could be here to meet you all," Catherine said suddenly, looking over her shoulder and gesturing for me to step forward. I did my best to resist and maintain my post at the back of the pack, but Catherine insisted. She took a step away from Charles to allow me to step forward between them, which left Charles looking visibly disheartened.

"It has been such a long time since I've been to Ridgewick," I said. "I'm glad to be back."

"Were you away?" Charles asked.

"In India," I said.

Charles' eyebrows shot up. "You've travelled a long way for a weekend in the country. What brought you back?"

I could feel everyone around me, aside from Charles, tense at his question. Vivian saved me from having to answer. She came to a dead stop in the middle of the path and turned on her brother. "Truly, it is shocking how little you concern yourself with the lives and affairs of our neighbors," she scolded.

This served only to confuse Charles further as he glanced from me to his sister and back again in search of some explanation. Vivian rolled her eyes.

"Her parents were murdered, brother. She has not come home for a weekend holiday, but because of the most horrific kind of trauma. I'm sure everyone would prefer you didn't mention the topic again."

Charles' cheeks went red and he turned to me, clearly prepared to make a grand apology that would draw the attention of the entire party and embarrass him and myself further. So, before he could open his mouth, I waved him away.

"I fear I did a poor job of keeping up with the London gossip while I was away, so I cannot fault you for being out of the loop, Charles," I said with a smile, hoping this would be the end of it.

Throughout the entire fiasco, Charles was so focused on the offense he may have caused me that Catherine was able to slip away unnoticed and take up position next to Mr. Matcham.

"You are too kind, Miss Beckingham," Charles said. "All of the Beckingham women are angels, both in demeanor and beauty."

Charles turned to where, moments before, Catherine had been standing, and his face fell when he saw her missing. He spun quickly and located her further up the trail with Mr. Matcham. His polite smile took a sharp turn downward, his eyebrows pulling together.

"I appreciate your understanding," he continued, less warmly than before. "Do excuse me."

With that, he walked briskly down the path in an attempt to catch up to Catherine and Mr. Matcham.

"Forgive my brother," Vivian said, shaking her head and pulling a reluctant Edward along with her. "He isn't one for social gossip. If it doesn't involve stocks or interest, he doesn't follow it."

I assured her I was not offended in the least, and it was true. The mention of the explosion in Simla had begun to have a less paralyzing affect on my thoughts. In the direct aftermath of the attack, I could hardly think about it without feeling the smoke in my lungs and seeing Rose's blood splattered on the leather. Now, however, I could discuss it without the trauma of the day consuming me.

I also wasn't offended because my thoughts were devoted elsewhere. The Chess Master had warned me there would be a murder, but I was not given any clue as to the motive or the method. All of my energy was focused on trying to solve the crime before it occurred. Seeing Charles pine for Catherine made me think the motive could be unrequited love. Clearly, Catherine wanted little to do with the man, and clearly Charles would not accept rejection without a fight. Could his spurned feelings lead him to murder? Was my cousin in mortal danger?

How would the Chess Master know of Charles' feelings, though? It would make more sense for the murder to be committed because of money or a personal vendetta, something that could be predicted long before it happened. Unrequited love would be a crime of passion, something no one could predict until the moment it happened. Was the Chess Master sophisticated enough to predict something as fickle as that?

The path moved to the east and then wrapped around the back of the property. Through a thick grove of trees, I was able to make out tiny scraps of the manicured garden that sat behind the house. Full-blossomed flowers filled the air with a fresh scent. I spotted thick flowering bushes along the wrought iron gate, primroses and stalks of lavender around a small circular pond in the center of the yard, and too many other flowers to count. It was a beautiful sight.

The path took a winding left turn, blocking the house from my view, and I used it as an opportunity to refocus on the guests in front of me. I couldn't afford to be distracted by wild accusations and theories. For all I knew, the murderer could be a stranger the Chess Master hired to sneak in during the night and kill someone at random, and not someone from the group at all. However, I could not control that. What I could do was try my utmost to ensure the killer was not one of Lord and Lady Ashton's guests, and to do that, I had to remain focused.

"Oh, Rose dear, we are not done catching up." Mrs.

Worthing appeared suddenly at my side. I hadn't even seen her approach, so I jumped violently. She laughed. "You are jumpy, dear. Though, I suppose, who can blame you? After everything that happened aboard the ship, you are right to be on edge."

"We ought not bring up that dreadful voyage," Mr. Worthing said, twisting his mustache between his fingers and studying a red-bellied bird in a nearby tree.

Mrs. Worthing cast her husband a withering look that he didn't notice and then turned her attention back to me. "Mr. Worthing doesn't like when I share the details of what happened on our voyage from India, but honestly, what does he expect me to talk about? It isn't every day you share such close quarters with a murderer."

I nearly laughed at her words. In most company, that would have been a perfectly accurate thing to say. It had not been my experience, however. It seemed as though murderers surrounded me wherever I went. And if the murderer the Chess Master warned me about was a member of the party, Mrs. Worthing had found herself close to one yet again.

"It's just that there are so many more cheerful things to discuss," Mr. Worthing said.

"You are right as ever, dear," Mrs. Worthing said, rolling her eyes playfully at me and sighing at her husband. "What have you done since we saw you last, Rose?"

"Well, I already told you about moving into my own home," I said.

"It has been weeks. Surely, you've been busy with other things, as well," she prodded.

I shook my head. "I'm afraid not. I've been occupied with preparing my home and organizing my staff."

I had been quite busy with other things, of course, but

nothing I wished to share with Mrs. Worthing. My insistence that I hadn't done anything noteworthy did not seem to convince Mrs. Worthing. She peppered me with questions about every restaurant I'd eaten at, every person I'd met, every building I'd stepped foot in. I answered her questions as succinctly as possible, avoiding mentioning The Chesney Ballroom and anyone I'd met who had somehow been involved in the murder of Frederick Grossmith.

"I'm sorry my stories aren't more interesting," I said, hoping to wrap up the conversation.

"Nonsense," Mrs. Worthing said. "You are young and single. Even your most mundane stories are the hottest gossip to the ears of a woman who has been married as long as I have."

Mr. Worthing startled at this, rousing out of his bird watching stupor. "We went out dancing just two weeks ago."

"You're right, dear," Mrs. Worthing said, running a hand down her husband's arm. "Our life is fascinating."

The two of them began to bicker as I mentally slipped away, taking notice of Dr. Shaw at the front of the group. He had been quite intrigued by Lord and Lady Ashton's tour at the start, but he seemed to be falling back, distancing himself. He was now in the middle of the group near Edward and Vivian, though I couldn't tell whether he was talking with them. Hoping to put some distance of my own between me and the Worthings, I quickened my pace.

Vivian was telling Edward about the lovely summer weather and how Somerset was the best place to experience it.

"It's so much more peaceful here than in the city. You can enjoy the days without being bombarded by noise and crowds. Out here, you can truly be alone," she said, tightening her grip on Edward's arm.

Speaking of being alone, it looked as though Edward wanted nothing more than to be alone at that moment. His gaze had been fixed firmly ahead, but when he saw Dr. Shaw moving towards him, he jumped at the chance to pair him off with the clingy Vivian.

"Vivian, have you met Dr. Shaw?" Edward asked. "Very interesting man."

Dr. Shaw jumped as though he'd forgotten he wasn't alone on the trail, and then introduced himself to Vivian Barry.

Vivian smiled uninterestedly. Just as Edward opened his mouth, probably so he could try to spark a conversation between Miss Barry and the doctor, Dr. Shaw bowed deeply and began backing away.

"I'm afraid I must cut the walk short and get back to the Hall. Lady Harwood has been alone for quite some time, and she can become anxious if I venture too far away. Please forgive my sudden exit," he said.

Everyone waved him farewell, Vivian smiling broadly at him, much more friendly than she had been only a moment before. As soon as the doctor was out of earshot, she turned to Edward. "He is rather tied to the old woman, isn't he?"

"He's her personal physician," Edward said coldly.

"You'd think he was her servant the way he caters to her," she said.

I turned to see Dr. Shaw nearly running up the trail towards the house and wondered whether Vivian hadn't touched on something. The old woman seemed to depend on him for everything. Perhaps he was growing tired of her demands and the constraints they placed on his own life. Perhaps he was unhappy enough to kill the old woman. The easier option, of course, would be to quit, but that could tarnish his reputation. As a personal physician, Dr. Shaw would want to be able to illustrate his utter devotion to his patients. And abandoning a sickly old woman near the end of her life would hardly look good. If Lady Harwood were to die, however, no one would find it suspicious. Especially if the method of murder was a subtle one.

The Beckinghams and their guests had continued on without me, everyone wrapped up in their own conversations—or, where Edward was concerned, consumed with thoughts of how to extract himself from his—and I walked down the path slowly, in no hurry to catch up to the party. I'd been at Ridgewick for less than an hour, and already I felt exhausted. Perhaps I should have taken Achilles Prideaux's advice and stayed away from the Chess Master's game. Of course, it was far too late for that. So, with a sigh, I quickened my pace and rejoined the Worthings, doing my best to answer Mrs. Worthing's incessant questions and keep one ear on the conversations happening around me.

7

O nce the trail wrapped back around to the front of the estate, I wasted no time breaking away from the ever-chatty Mrs. Worthing and sneaking away to my room for the weekend, both to unpack and relax. Trying to maintain a façade of normalcy while also suspecting everyone around me of being a murderer or of being murdered very soon was incredibly exhausting.

My room was on an upper floor, just at the top of a large wooden staircase, and in the direct center of a long hallway of guest bedrooms. My room looked perfectly in order—the pillow had been recently fluffed and the drapes were drawn open—but there was a lingering scent of dust, verifying my suspicion that the Beckinghams did not visit the house very often.

A maid had already unpacked my small suitcase, arranging my shoes near each of the dresses that might pair well with them over the weekend. Looking at the clothing that hung waiting for me, I thought not for the first time that shallow concerns such as what clothes I would be wearing seemed entirely insignificant in the face of someone losing their life. But still, murder or not, I had to carry on as always. Life didn't stop moving for anyone.

When I made it back downstairs, everyone was in the sitting room in anticipation of dinner beginning soon. A servant with snow white hair and a matching mustache was making drinks. I requested a martini and took the seat on the couch next to Lady Ashton.

"The estate is so fascinating," Dr. Shaw said as he positioned Lady Harwood's wheelchair next to the sofa. "I cannot wait to finish the second half of the tour."

"Oh, it is much like the first half," Lord Ashton said with a laugh.

"Except, you did miss the walk through of the south garden," Lady Ashton said. "I can show it to you after dinner."

"I would enjoy that," Dr. Shaw said.

"I need my medicine after dinner," Lady Harwood piped up, holding a shaking hand into the air to draw the doctor's attention.

"Of course, Lady Harwood. I will see the garden once I have administered your medication," he said gently. This seemed enough to calm the old woman's worries, and she sunk back into her wheelchair.

Lady Ashton smiled awkwardly and continued. "The gardens are my favorite part of the entire property. They are becoming harder and harder to upkeep, but it is so worth it."

Lord Ashton barked out a laugh. "Hardly. The expense of everything seems to rise by the hour. We've had three different gardeners within the year, each expecting higher wages than the last. It's outrageous."

"It can be expensive, but I just can't fathom leaving the gardens to nature," Lady Ashton said. "It would be such a shame."

"Prices in the area do seem much higher than they once were," Dr. Shaw agreed. "Many large estates that have been with the same families for generations are being broken up. It seems to be a hard time for everyone."

Charles Barry, who had been nodding along throughout the whole conversation, finally voiced his agreement. "The countryside has been noticeably less occupied this summer than in previous years."

Mr. Matcham, from where he stood next to the fireplace, let out a *humph* of disagreement. "If people are losing their family estates, I have to think that is more of a personal fault than anything to do with the economy."

Everyone in the room, aside from Catherine who was standing on the opposite side of the fireplace, her eyes fixed on Mr. Matcham, seemed uncomfortable with his words, yet he continued.

"I don't like to speak publicly about my personal accounts and affairs, but my finances have never looked better. It is all about knowing how to adapt and when to strike," he said, seeming to have no issue discussing his personal accounts in the slightest.

The room went silent, no one quite sure how to smooth away the awkwardness. Mr. Matcham was the only person who didn't seem to notice. He smiled at Catherine, and though she smiled back, I could tell it was slightly strained. Lord Ashton had gone red-faced and I could only imagine the flurry of unspoken words swirling around inside of him. With the Beckingham's own financial situation recently becoming less prosperous than it once was, I suspected my uncle took a particularly dim view of Mr. Matcham's careless attitude. Thankfully, before the silence could stretch on too long, Lady Ashton rose to her feet and clapped her hands twice.

"It is just about time for dinner, so we can all move to the dining room. We're very informal here, so you must feel free to seat yourselves however you like."

The table was set with beautiful gold-edged china, crystal drinking glasses, and freshly shined silver. I moved to a chair near the end of the table just as Mr. Matcham pulled out the chair next to it. Before I could sit down, however, Lady Ashton called to me.

"I'd love if you could sit next to me, Rose," Lady Ashton said with a calm smile. When I was standing next to her, she leaned in to whisper in my ear. "Best to avoid Mr. Matcham."

I wanted to ask why, but she was already engaging Vivian Barry in conversation about the origins of the dishware.

Group conversation was spurned in favor of several small conversations amongst the guests. Catherine was torn between the men on either side of her, Mr. Matcham and Charles. Lord and Lady Ashton spoke almost exclusively with the Worthings, but Lady Ashton seemed incapable of focusing on anything other than her daughter sitting next to the man she had pulled me away from. Edward had not been successful in ridding himself of Vivian, and Dr. Shaw devoted himself to helping Lady Harwood cut her meat between bites of his own meal.

As servants carried dinner away and dessert—a sweet bread with cold cream and fruit—was brought out, I leaned in to Lady Ashton.

"Why is it best to avoid Mr. Matcham?" I whispered. The man had obviously offended everyone by bragging of his wealth in the sitting room, but it seemed as though there had been a negative opinion of him from the moment of his arrival, and I wanted to understand why.

Lady Ashton looked around sharply to be sure we weren't being overheard. "His fortune was made through gambling and speculation. He speaks of his business prowess, but the man runs with an unsavory crowd and does little to hide it."

"Why was he invited here this weekend?" I asked.

Lady Ashton sighed. "As much as we may have wanted to lose his invitation in the post, it felt wrong to invite our other neighbors without extending the courtesy to Mr. Matcham, as well. He is often out of town on *business* or unable to attend, but his schedule was open this weekend."

"The things one does in the name of etiquette," I said.

Lady Ashton laughed quietly. "Yes, indeed."

As soon as dessert was finished, the gentlemen move to the drawing room under the pretense of an after-dinner smoke. However, when the ladies joined them several minutes later, a game of cards seemed to have been the true purpose. Mr. Matcham, Charles Barry, Edward, and Lord Ashton were all gathered around a small table in the corner, hunched over as if they could block their activity from the eyes of the encroaching ladies.

"You are not turning our respectable home into a place of gambling and debauchery, are you, my dear?" Lady Ashton asked her husband. Her words were playful, but her eyes focused pointedly on Mr. Matcham.

"Never, darling," Lord Ashton responded, eliciting a chuckle from the men.

Mr. Worthing had apparently decided to skip the game of cards and he spoke up to quell Lady Ashton's worries. "I've been keeping an eye on the gentlemen for you. I won't let things get out of hand."

Lady Ashton gave him a genuine smile in return.

"You are all of fine breeding," Mr. Matcham said loudly,

holding his hand of cards against his chest. "I suspect your tolerance for debauchery is much lower than mine."

"Are you not of fine breeding, as well?" Lady Ashton asked, head quirked to the side.

"Not as fine as some," Mr. Matcham responded, his mouth pulled up in a satisfied smirk.

It was difficult to read the tension between my aunt and her guest, but it was clear each knew of the other's dislike for them, which led me to wonder whether someone in my own family couldn't be the murderer. I tried to imagine Lady Ashton killing Mr. Matcham over his poor reputation or the subtle disrespect he'd shown her, but the image wouldn't come. She was a gentle woman and could not be capable of something so heinous.

Lady Ashton laughed and took a seat on the sofa, patting the cushion next to her for me to claim. "I suppose we all could say the same, Mr. Matcham."

"Quite true," Charles said, smiling broadly at Catherine as she entered. "Social class hardly matters when you consider we are all beneath someone else."

I didn't know Charles and Vivian well enough to have any idea of their fortune or standing in society, but I could hazard a guess and assumed they were not as well off as the Beckinghams. This discrepancy in their social standing was most likely the inspiration behind Charles's statement. Anyone with eyes could see he found it difficult to tear his away from Catherine. Unfortunately for Charles, anyone with eyes could also see Catherine did not have any for him.

"That idea only works when you are in good company, brother," Vivian said, moving along the outer edge of the room until she came to stand behind Edward's chair. She placed her hands lightly on the wood back of it, her fingers hovering over his shoulders. "In many areas of London, social class matters a great deal. We are all lower than some-one, but some are lower than everyone."

Edward hunched forward over the card table, and Vivian frowned and folded her hands behind her back. I glanced at the Worthings to see whether all the talk of social class was making them uncomfortable, but they were both busy examining a painted porcelain dish at the center of a low table nearby and weren't paying any mind to the conver-sation at all.

"You've put in too much money, Matcham," Edward said.

"Have I?" he asked. "I didn't realize we'd set a limit."

"There is always a limit in friendly games." Edward's dark eyes were narrowed, his hair curling down onto his forehead and casting a long shadow down his cheeks.

"If you are not comfortable with the amount then I can take it back," Mr. Matcham said, hand hovering over the center of the table. Then, his voice lowered. "I wouldn't want to make anyone financially uneasy."

Edward sat up straight and shook his head. "No, I'm fine. I just didn't want you to risk more than you could handle."

The game continued, the gentlemen becoming consider-ably more tense with each passing hand. Charles' pale face turned a nasty shade of red and Lord Ashton seemed to be in a war between his good judgment and supporting his only son—I suspected he would have bowed out of the game much sooner had Edward not been playing.

Lady Ashton did her best to steer the party's attention to talk of more cheerful things.

"Haven't you found this summer to be one of the loveliest in recent memory, Lady Harwood?"

The old woman was sitting near the unlit fireplace, a blanket wrapped around her legs. She shook her head before Lady Ashton had even finished her sentence. "The heat gives me splitting headaches and my joints ache."

"I'm sorry to hear that," Lady Ashton said, recovering quickly. "I thought it was the cold that usually disrupted joints."

"Both heat and cold can cause aches when you are as old as I am," she said sourly. "Dr. Shaw, I think I'd like to go to my room now."

The doctor had just sat down after adjusting her blanket, so it wouldn't cover her feet and "stifle" her, but he dutifully stood back up and rolled her out of the room and down the hallway. Lady Harwood had been given a room on the ground floor because of her wheelchair, and she had requested that Dr. Shaw take the room just next door in case she should need him in the night.

"Thank you for a pleasant evening," Dr. Shaw said.

"Goodnight," Lady Ashton called. "Breakfast will be at seven, and we all take it together in the dining room."

No sooner had the old woman and her doctor disappeared around the corner, than the card table erupted in shouts.

"You cheated!"

"I've won!"

"Liar!"

All the men at the table, save for Mr. Matcham, had risen to their feet. They were breathing heavily and staring down at the man with narrowed eyes and closed fists. If I was Mr. Matcham, I would have been quite uncomfortable, but he looked perfectly at ease.

"Good game, fellows," he said, sweeping the money in the center of the table towards himself.

"This isn't...right," Charles stuttered.

Edward's upper lip was pulled back in a snarl. "You're a cheat. A no-good cheat."

"A no-good cheat?" Mr. Matcham repeated, a hint of pleasure in his tone. "I'd always considered myself a very *good* cheat."

"Matcham," Lord Ashton warned, placing his hand on his son's chest to keep him from lunging across the table at the man.

"I'm only joking, Ashton. You saw the game. I didn't cheat," Mr. Matcham said as he gathered his winnings and stood up. I'd almost forgotten how tall Mr. Matcham was, but now that the men at the table looked to be preparing for a fight, I couldn't help but notice how he towered over the others.

"Of course he didn't cheat." Catherine had grabbed a book from the shelf and taken a seat in the corner of the room as soon as she entered. I'd suspected the entire evening that she wasn't reading so much as she was giving off the appearance of reading to avoid a conversation with Charles Barry. Now, she closed the book and left it on the chair where she'd been sitting as she crossed the room to stand behind Mr. Matcham, facing off against her own father and brother. "We are all friends here. Why would he cheat?"

"Catherine, stay out of this," Edward snapped.

"Mr. Matcham is our friend, brother, and has been for many years. You owe him an apology."

Edward looked prepared to break the table over his knee and hit Mr. Matcham on the head with the pieces.

"I don't wish to offend you, dear Catherine, but you did not have a good vantage point from that chair in the corner," Charles Barry said, surprising everyone, Catherine included.

"If my winning has upset you all, then I will gladly return your money," Mr. Matcham said as he tucked his winnings even more snuggly inside the inner pocket of his suit jacket. "I was under the belief that everyone was betting only what they could afford to lose. If that isn't the case, I'd hate to be the reason anyone faced financial discomfort."

Mr. Matcham was a clever man. If anyone accepted their money back now, they would have to admit to being in dire financial straits, and that was something no one, especially in present company, would want to admit to.

"I think Mr. Worthing and I will head upstairs now," Mrs. Worthing said uncomfortably, hauling Mr. Worthing out of his chair by his elbow.

"Perhaps we should all retire," Lady Ashton said, shooting a sharp look at her husband. "It has been a long day."

The men at the table continued to stare at one another, and it was clear the situation would either dissolve or come to blows. Everyone in the room waited on baited breath to see which one it would be. Finally, Lord Ashton sighed and stepped away from the table. "Yes, it is getting late. It would be best for us all to get some sleep after our day of travel."

Edward snapped his head towards his father, a look of betrayal in his eyes. Just as quickly as it appeared, he wiped it away, returning his face to one of cool indifference. "Good-night, everyone. Sorry if I played any part in ruining your evening."

Mrs. Worthing laughed and took several more stumbling steps towards the door. "Nonsense. No one's evening was ruined."

"Of course, not," Lady Ashton said.

Charles took a long look at Catherine and deflated when

she stood resolutely behind Mr. Matcham's chair, avoiding his gaze. "Shall we turn in, as well, Vivian?"

Charles stepped out from behind the card table and linked arms with his sister.

Lord Ashton, satisfied the situation was under control, offered Lady Ashton a hand to escort her upstairs for the evening. Everyone else followed suit, heading for the wide doorway that opened into the entrance hall.

Just as my feet touched the bottom of the staircase, I heard a chuckle from the room behind me. I turned to see Mr. Matcham leaning against the doorway, arms crossed over his chest. When he saw he had my attention, he winked. "Don't worry, Miss Beckingham. Tempers will have cooled by morning. Everything will be better tomorrow."

Not sure what to say, I gave the man a smile and followed my family up to the next floor. Once inside my room, I locked the door behind me. I could only hope everyone else in the house had the good sense to do the same.

8

L ady Ashton had announced the night before when breakfast would start, but her guests apparently took no notice. Myself and the immediate Beckingham family were all sitting at the table, surrounded by platters of food brought out by a pair of male servants, but the seats reserved for each of the guests sat empty.

I wondered whether everyone had slept as restlessly as I had. I'd tossed and turned all night, imagining I heard footsteps in the hallway, my doorknob turning slowly. I saw looming figures in every shadow in my room and had to throw the curtains wide to illuminate the room with moonlight. When I wasn't concerned for my own safety, I had my ear pressed to the door, trying to decide which, if any, of the guests at Ridgewick Hall could be the murderer's victim.

Seeing the Ashton family assembled at the table was a welcome sight. It meant they had all survived the night.

"Did I miss anything last night?" Alice asked grumpily. Her mother had sent her to bed after dinner, which with the chaos that erupted, had proven to be a good decision.

"Not a thing," Edward said coolly.

It appeared Mr. Matcham was wrong about tempers cooling overnight. Edward looked just as angry as he had when he'd gone to bed.

"Just boring adult conversation," Lord Ashton said.

Alice mumbled under her breath about being nearly an adult, but no one heard her as the Worthings came downstairs and entered the dining room. Mr. Worthing was remarking on the fine craftsmanship of the banisters and Mrs. Worthing was asking whether her dress had zipped up all the way in the back.

Lady Ashton hid an amused smile. Just as I had aboard the *RMS Star of India*, I knew Lady Ashton was finding herself smitten with the older couple. Despite their faults and clumsy social graces, they were undeniably charming.

"How did you both sleep?" Lord Ashton asked as the couple came into the dining room.

"Quite well. My bed was remarkably comfortable," Mrs. Worthing said. "Like sleeping on a cloud."

No sooner had the Worthings taken their seats than Lady Harwood and Dr. Shaw appeared from the side hallway. Lord Ashton asked Lady Harwood the same question but received a much different response.

"Not well," she said, shaking her head, her cold eyes looking towards the ceiling. "Not well at all. I spent most of the night in a fever of some kind. Dr. Shaw had to apply cool rags to my forehead."

Now that Lady Harwood mentioned it, Dr. Shaw looked haggard. Dark circles pooled under his eyes and his cheeks hung from his bones like wet sheets over a line.

As Lady Ashton attended to Lady Harwood, letting the old woman complain about her aches and pains, giving Dr. Shaw a much-needed break, the Barry siblings strolled through the door, arm in arm as always.

"Good morning, everyone," Charles greeted us cheerily, seeming to have shrugged off the botched card game of the night before in a way Edward had not. "Sorry we are late. Did everyone sleep well?"

There was a mumbled response.

"And you, Catherine?" he asked, claiming the seat next to my cousin. "Did you sleep well?"

Catherine quickly filled her mouth with a forkful of fresh fruit and then smiled at him, nodding her head.

I couldn't understand Catherine's complete dismissal of Charles Barry. He was a cheerful man, certainly, and Catherine had always been more on the cynical side, but he came from a good family and seemed to be affable, at the very least. And I knew many women, myself included, who would find him quite handsome.

Lord Ashton clapped his hands, quieting the conversations at the table. "Well, we are still short one guest, but I'm sure Mr. Matcham wouldn't mind if we began without him."

Breakfast was a full English. Two eggs with round yellow yolks in the center, two links of sausage, crispy toast with generous dollops of butter, baked beans, and seasoned slices of tomato that Lady Ashton announced were taken from the estate's own garden. Very little conversation happened over breakfast. Everyone was much too busy eating and refilling their plates. I'd had a nervous stomach all morning, but even I couldn't resist the salty, savory scent of the food before me.

It wasn't until breakfast was winding down that anyone made mention of Mr. Matcham again.

"Should someone go and knock on his door?" Mrs. Worthing asked, already nudging her husband to volunteer.

"I'm sure he'll come down when he is ready," Charles said.

"He's probably counting his money," Edward mumbled just loud enough for myself and Lady Ashton to hear him. She gave her son a stern look and then smiled at her husband.

"Perhaps we ought to send a servant to make sure he is awake," she suggested. "I'd hate for his breakfast to get cold."

Before Lord Ashton could respond, Lady Harwood coughed violently and then shook her head. "Perhaps Mr. Matcham came down with the same illness that plagued me last night. If that is the case, Dr. Shaw ought to go up and check on him."

"I'd be happy to look in on him," Catherine said quickly.

Lord Ashton shook his head at his daughter, even as Lady Harwood froze her with one withering glare.

Dr. Shaw knew his employer had won the argument and dutifully stood and marched out of the room.

"I hope Mr. Matcham isn't ill," Lady Ashton said after several long seconds of silence.

"I hope it isn't contagious," Edward mumbled.

I hoped Edward wouldn't be in a dark mood all weekend because of the card game. Why would he choose to gamble if he didn't want to lose any money?

When Dr. Shaw's absence stretched unexpectedly long, Lady Ashton made some joke about Mr. Matcham being a heavy sleeper.

A few more minutes passed and then echoing sounds reached the dining room, the drumming of heavy, pounding footsteps moving down the staircase at a startling speed, as if the doctor were running.

Everyone at the table exchanged glances at the sound of the frantic approach, as if we all sensed something was wrong. My aunt was the first one to stand up and make her way into the entrance hall.

By the time I stood from my seat and hurried out of the dining room after her, Dr. Shaw was already reaching the foot of the stairs. His face had turned a sickly shade of yellow except for rosy splotches across his cheeks from his sprint down the stairs. He came to a sliding stop on the tile floor of the entrance hall, his chest heaving with exertion, and shouted.

"HE'S DEAD!"

I hadn't even contemplated the idea that Mr. Matcham could be the murder victim the Chess Master had warned me about. He was a large man, both tall and wide, and he looked like someone who had been in his fair share of fights. If I were a murderer, he would have been my absolute last choice of victim. So, when Mr. Matcham failed to show up for breakfast, I had simply thought he'd chosen to sleep in. Or, rather, to avoid the men he had cheated out of money the evening before. Murder had been the last thought in my mind.

There was a collective gasp from the other guests who had clustered behind me and then the room froze, everyone waiting for someone else to make the first move.

"Get your medical bag," Lady Harwood shouted, pointing at Dr. Shaw.

The man seemed to remember all at once that he was a doctor, and he disappeared down the long hallway only to return with a large black bag beating against his calf. He didn't stop in the entrance hall but ran straight up the stairs and pounded back down the hallway. This time, I followed him.

Lord and Lady Ashton were just behind me. Lord Ashton said something about the ladies not seeing the body, but I didn't listen. I had to see Mr. Matcham. If he was the victim the Chess Master had referred to, I had to solve the case. I had to discover who the murderer was. If I couldn't stop the murder from happening, at least I could gain the promised reward.

Dr. Shaw disappeared inside Mr. Matcham's open door as I reached the top of the stairs. I moved down the hallway slowly, both wanting and not wanting to make it to Mr. Matcham's door. I'd seen enough dead bodies in the preceding months to last me a lifetime. Several lifetimes, in fact. But still, I would have to see one more.

The curtains were drawn tightly and Mr. Matcham looked as if he could have been sleeping, as I pushed the door open and stepped into the room. Except, Mr. Matcham would not be rousing from this slumber. As I got closer, his lips were circled in a shade of icy blue that matched his hands, which were folded on top of the blankets. He looked perfectly arranged. No apparent signs of a fight or a struggle.

Dr. Shaw placed a stethoscope to Mr. Matcham's chest in the name of being thorough and shook his head when he heard nothing.

"How long has he been dead?" Lady Ashton asked from near the door. I hadn't heard her or Lord Ashton walk in behind me.

Dr. Shaw touched the back of his hand to Mr. Matcham's cheek. "A few hours, maybe longer. He's completely cold."

I noticed Lady Ashton didn't ask how Mr. Matcham died, so I did.

"It's hard to say," Dr. Shaw said, the nerves I saw in the entrance hall fading into routine. He had seen considerably more dead bodies than I had, I'd wager. Mr. Matcham had turned from a fallen guest to a patient. "No wounds, his eyes are not bloodshot, and nothing looked out of the ordinary when I arrived."

"Are you ruling out foul play?" I asked.

He nodded. "I believe so. If I had to guess, I'd say this was a violent heart attack. It killed him suddenly."

"Isn't he a little young for a heart attack?" I asked.

"He led a rough lifestyle," Lady Ashton said. "Drinking, and there were rumors of dangerous drugs. Would that contribute to an early heart attack, Doctor?"

"It could," Dr. Shaw said. "It can also run in a family. Do either of you know anything about his parents?"

"Nothing," Lord Ashton said, wrapping his arm around his wife's shoulders. "He has been our neighbor for years, but we were not friendly. Of course, we invited him to the estate this weekend, but we extended an invitation to all of the neighbors. It was a courtesy. I suppose we should call the police, shouldn't we? Someone should know this has happened."

I couldn't remember ever hearing Lord Ashton so flustered. His eyes were darting back and forth and he just kept talking.

"I've already told Burton to telephone the police," Edward said, interrupting his father's ramble and making everyone in the room jump at his entrance.

I assumed the "Burton" he spoke of was the head butler, a stout, white-haired servant I'd seen around the house.

When Edward saw Mr. Matcham, his face went pale. "So, it's true, then?"

"I'm afraid so," Dr. Shaw said. "A suspected heart attack."

I stepped closer to the bed, knowing I wouldn't have another opportunity once the authorities arrived. Dr. Shaw was right. There didn't appear to be a single sign of struggle. No bruising or scratches. No defensive wounds. Even with the Chess Master's warning flashing in my mind, I had to wonder whether Mr. Matcham's death wasn't a coincidence. I studied his lifeless face and trailed my gaze down each of his arms before I noticed the tiniest inconsistency on his otherwise perfect skin. A small prick near his wrist.

"What is that mark from?" I asked, pointing towards his arm, careful not to touch him.

Dr. Shaw leaned in closer and squinted. "It looks like a type of insect bite."

"That would make sense," Edward said. "We were outside a good deal yesterday."

"It seems to be the only one on his entire body," I said. "And I don't have any similar bites on mine."

"I'll be sure to point it out to the authorities when they arrive," Dr. Shaw said. "Perhaps, we should clear the room until then."

I nodded, content with Dr. Shaw's answer. The authorities would know whether the mark was anything to be concerned about. Their response would tell me whether this was the murder I was meant to solve or whether there would be yet another before the weekend was out.

C atherine had been a mess since the moment we'd returned downstairs with confirmation that Mr. Matcham was deceased.

"How did he die? When? Did he suffer?" she asked, alternating between pacing the length of the dining room and collapsing down into the chair Mr. Matcham would have sat in if he'd made it to breakfast.

Dr. Shaw relayed all the information he had but kept insisting that everyone should wait for the authorities.

"Do you believe Mr. Matcham was murdered?" I asked, unable to stop myself.

Not until I saw the startled expressions of everyone around me did I realize this was an abnormal assumption to leap to, from most people's perspectives.

"No, he does not believe that," Lord Ashton said firmly, answering for Dr. Shaw. "At this point, we have no reason to suspect anyone was murdered."

Except for the letter I received several days ago that said someone in the Somerset countryside would be murdered, I thought. It seemed like too big of a coincidence that Mr.

Matcham would die suddenly in his sleep at the same time someone was meant to be murdered. However, if Dr. Shaw thought his death was brought on by natural causes, who was I to disagree? He was a medical professional. The bite mark on Mr. Matcham's wrist had seemed suspicious, but it also could have just been a bite mark. The Chess Master's warning could have been causing me to see clues where there weren't any.

"Can I see him?" Catherine asked, moving towards the entrance hall.

Her mother reached out and stopped her. "I don't think that is a good idea, Cat. We should wait for the police."

"He's all alone up there," Catherine said.

"He's been alone up there for hours," Edward said.

Everyone's attention turned to him. Lady Ashton narrowed her eyes at her son and Catherine looked on the verge of sobbing.

"That's what Dr. Shaw said." Edward shrugged. It was strange to see him even the slightest bit repentant. "I just mean, Mr. Matcham no longer minds being alone."

"We don't know how he died yet," Charles said, moving to stand between Edward and Catherine. "He could be infectious and spread something to you."

At this, Catherine's nose wrinkled. She looked slightly less sad and a bit more disgusted. Dr. Shaw folded his hands self-consciously behind his back, and I suddenly felt myself itching for a bar of soap.

"We have no reason to believe he is infectious," Lady Ashton said, calming the worry everyone could sense building in the room. "Dr. Shaw suggested it could have been a heart attack. With Mr. Matcham's unsavory lifestyle, it isn't out of the question. But we won't know anything for certain until the authorities arrive."

"The police will be *here*?" Alice asked a bit too excitedly.

I could see Lady Ashton growing weary of her children. Between Catherine's stifled sobs, Edward's snide remarks, and now Alice's inappropriate excitement, I knew she was only a few minutes away from snapping. Intervening, I pulled Alice into my side and rubbed her shoulder.

"Yes, the police will be here, but we will have to stand back and let them do their work," I said.

Alice stood on her toes and whispered. "Can I see the body?"

"NO! You cannot see the body," Catherine exploded. "He isn't a side show for you to ogle."

"You wanted to go up and sit with it," Alice snapped back, arms crossed over her chest.

"He is a *HE*, Alice. Not an *IT*," Catherine shouted.

"I'm going to call for some drinks," Lord Ashton said.

"It's morning, dear—"

Lord Ashton held up a hand to cut off his wife. "Special circumstances."

Wine and brandy were offered and nearly everyone, except for Alice, accepted a drink. Even Lady Harwood sipped a small amount of wine. Under normal circumstances, she probably would have refused, but Mr. Matcham's death seemed to have rattled her. She'd made the suggestion that morning that perhaps he'd been ill with whatever she'd had the night before, and I was fairly certain she now believed a similar death could come for her at any moment. The impromptu examination she demanded for herself saved Dr. Shaw from the endless questions the guests had about his brief examination of the dead man.

"Did Mr. Matcham seem ill last night?" Mrs. Worthing asked after her second glass of wine. "I don't recall him looking unwell at all."

"Heart attacks can come on quite suddenly," Mr. Worthing said. "It's why they are called 'attacks.'"

He found this to be a rather funny joke but stopped laughing when Mrs. Worthing elbowed him in the side.

"He looked to be in fine health last night," I said, trying to gauge the reactions of the rest of the party. Everyone had seemed equally surprised at the news of his death, but only Catherine seemed genuinely distraught. In fact, Catherine had been the only person at Ridgewick Hall to act as if she liked Mr. Matcham when he was alive. Everyone else seemed to simply tolerate him.

Lady Ashton had been displeased with Mr. Matcham's presence all weekend. She'd even gone so far as to keep me from sitting next to him at dinner. Edward had definitely taken the loss of the card game to heart. He was convinced Mr. Matcham cheated him out of his money. Charles' affections for Catherine put him at direct odds with Mr. Matcham because of the spell the other man had managed to cast over Catherine. And Mr. Matcham's general attitude was enough for me to guess he had plenty of enemies outside of Ridgewick Hall. If he had been murdered, the list of suspects would undoubtedly be a long one.

"Is our resident detective going to have to solve another murder case?" Mrs. Worthing asked, winking at me and nearly sloshing her drink on the carpet.

Dr. Shaw had been enjoying a rare moment of peace since Lady Harwood had managed to doze into a mid-morning nap, but that ended as soon as Catherine spun towards him, arms waving accusatorily. "I thought you said Mr. Matcham wasn't murdered. You said he died of a heart attack. You said he died of natural causes."

Catherine was closing in on the poor man. He looked up at her, horrified, and I couldn't blame him. Catherine was a lovely woman, but after so many tears and silent sobs, her eyes were red and puffy, her cheeks streaked with salty tears, her lips nearly bloody from where she'd been chewing them.

Dr. Shaw held up his hands to hold her off as though he was afraid she would lunge out and attack him. I wasn't convinced she wouldn't. Catherine seemed several notches short of stable.

"Mrs. Worthing was joking," I said, trying to grab my cousin's attention. "She was teasing me."

Catherine froze and then spun towards me, redirecting her anger. "What kind of a joke is that? It doesn't sound like a joke. Are you all lying to me?"

"Why would we lie to you, Cat?" Lady Ashton asked. "You have the same information as everyone else. No one is lying."

I didn't think Mrs. Worthing capable of embarrassment, but her face was a violent shade of red. "Yes, dear, it was a poor attempt at humor. I'm so sorry to have offended you. I didn't realize you were close with the man."

"I wasn't," Catherine snapped. "Close with him, that is. But if there is a murderer in our midst, I'd like to know. We all would have a right to know."

"There is no murderer," Edward said, stepping forward and rubbing a hand across his sister's shoulder. "Everyone is understandably tense. We just need to relax."

This seemed to ease Catherine, but then Vivian stood up and cleared her throat. "What did Mrs. Worthing mean about Rose being our resident detective?"

I held back a groan.

"There was a murder aboard the ship we took from Bombay to London," Mrs. Worthing said excitedly. "And Rose discovered the identity of the killer."

Vivian raised an eyebrow and looked at me. "You solved a murder?"

"And another one a few weeks ago," Edward added absentmindedly. "A bartender at a jazz club was killed, and Rose was a witness."

"I wasn't a witness exactly," I tried to correct. "It was a misunderstanding."

"But you investigated that matter, too?" she asked.

I knew it would look suspicious. Murder seemed to follow me around. If I was anyone else, I'd suspect me, too. "I'm not a detective," I said. "I asked some questions, followed some clues. It was nothing."

Vivian pursed her lips, and I could see the thoughts forming behind her eyes. If the authorities arrived and declared Mr. Matcham to have been murdered, my name would be the first one to cross Vivian's lips.

Before anyone could respond or change the subject, the butler appeared, announcing that the police had arrived.

The rest of the morning passed in a flurry of activity. People were moving up and down the stairs, tromping down the hallway to Mr. Matcham's room and back again. Strange voices floated through the house, filling the nearly silent sitting room where most of us had settled. Lord and Lady Ashton helped direct the officers through the house and gave statements, but I caught them whispering to one another about whether to send everyone home and cancel the weekend.

"This has been traumatic," Lady Ashton argued. "We all need the support of being together."

"A man has died, dear."

"Exactly. More reason to stay here and make sense of it before we send our shocked guests back into the world. Besides, I am certain the police will want us all where we can be easily reached should they have any questions over the next day or two."

I didn't get to hear their final decision because just then an officer called my uncle away to ask whether there was another, more discreet staircase they could use to remove the body.

When I went back to the sitting room, Dr. Shaw had pulled himself away from Lady Harwood and taken up position in front of a bookshelf in the corner. He had a heavy leather-bound book in his hands, so he didn't notice when I approached him.

"Interesting morning, doctor," I said.

He jumped slightly, closing the book suddenly. "Yes, more interesting than most."

"Most? Do you do this kind of thing often?" I asked.

"Well, I'm a personal physician," he said by way of explanation, but upon seeing my lack of understanding, he continued. "Normally, only those who are already rather ill need a doctor always on hand. So, my employers are predisposed to dying suddenly."

"Oh, right. Of course," I said, feeling daft. "Between you and me, Lady Harwood doesn't seem all that ill."

"She is an elderly woman," he said, shifting his feet, and looking around to be sure Lady Harwood wasn't within hearing distance. "But if you are suggesting she isn't in dire need of a personal physician, then I'd have to agree. The woman may outlive me."

We laughed and then settled into a comfortable quiet. "Dr. Shaw, may I ask you a question?"

"Of course, Miss Beckingham," he said warmly.

"The mark on Mr. Matcham's arm," I said, leaning in so as not to be overheard. "Do you truly believe it to be an insect bite?"

He nodded immediately. "I do. Are you not convinced?"

"Not entirely," I admitted. "It was a single puncture and there didn't appear to be any irritation around the site."

"Not all insect bites cause a histamine reaction," he said.

"And most needle injection sites could be mistaken for insect bites," I said quietly, eyebrows raised.

Dr. Shaw's face turned stony. "You believe he was poisoned?"

"I'm not sure. That's why I'm asking you. Are there any medications that could kill someone instantly?"

"Why instantly?" he asked, eyebrows furrowed.

"Mr. Matcham was a large man. If he'd felt the injection going in, he would have fought. Everyone in the house would have heard him shouting and we would have run to his room. If the killer wanted to escape, they would have had to kill him instantly."

Dr. Shaw seemed to think on this. So long, in fact, that I began to wonder whether he wasn't willfully ignoring me, hoping I'd go away. After several minutes he leaned in and whispered. "There are some fast-acting tranquilizers that, in high enough doses, can be lethal. Depending on the dosage, Mr. Matcham could have succumbed to the medicine before there was time to struggle. But those medications are very difficult to come by. No ordinary person would have access."

Just then, Dr. Shaw seemed to understand the implication of what he was saying and shook his head. "But you must know, Miss Beckingham, that I would never harm a soul. If that is why you've come to talk to me, to try and gather evidence against me, then I must warn you that I do not look kindly on it. You may fancy yourself a resident detective, but I will not have my reputation questioned because of the opinion of a young woman with no medical expertise."

Dr. Shaw had been a quiet, subdued man since I'd first met him, so his sudden anger shocked me. I stepped back and blinked, trying to calm myself before I continued.

"Doctor, I never suggested a thing, I assure you. I only came to ask whether you thought it possible the insect bite could be more than a bite? I'm sorry if there was any miscommunication."

Dr. Shaw straightened up and ran a finger under his shirt collar. "In that case, forgive me. It's been a stressful morning. To answer your question, no, I do not believe the puncture is an injection site. I believe it is a small insect bite Mr. Matcham acquired sometime yesterday while we were out of doors."

I thanked Dr. Shaw for his time and turned away just as Lady Ashton came into the sitting room, arms raised to gain everyone's attention. "Mr. Matcham's body has been removed, and although we will not know the cause until there has been an official examination, it appears his death was entirely natural."

Everyone in the room seemed to sigh in relief.

"Well," Lord Ashton said. "Now that's settled, I think we all need some sustenance. I'm sure everyone's appetites are low, after the events of this morning, but it's important to keep up our strength. With that in mind, tea has been arranged outdoors. Shall we retire to the garden?"

Catherine stood up abruptly, let out a loud sob, and ran from the room.

10

Try as everyone might to go on as normal, the weekend had taken a decidedly somber tone. Catherine could hardly get through ten minutes without hiccupping and excusing herself to cry. Charles usually followed after her, though he would undoubtedly return a minute later, claiming Catherine needed to be alone. Edward grew more cross each time Catherine broke down in a fit of emotion. And Lord and Lady Ashton insisted on moving forward as though nothing had happened. I wasn't sure which reaction was worse: Catherine's unending sadness or her parents' immutable cheerfulness.

During afternoon tea in the garden, Lady Harwood was regaling everyone with a tale of the last time Mr. Matcham had visited her home.

"The man couldn't go a single evening without attempting to win himself money somewhere," she said, her tone toeing the line between criticism and amusement. "He harassed poor Dr. Shaw to no end to go in with him on whatever mad business venture he was pursuing at the time."

"Did you go in with him, Dr. Shaw?" Vivian asked.

Dr. Shaw shook his head, but before he could say anything, Lady Harwood let out a bark of laughter. "Of course not. No fool would do business with Mr. Matcham. I know we shouldn't speak ill of the dead, but he was a horrendous businessman."

Catherine had only just returned from a crying fit, but that didn't seem to matter. Her face puckered, and she burst into tears once again, running through the grass up to the house. Charles rose to follow her, but Lady Ashton held him back.

"She may be in need of womanly company," she said. "Rose, would you mind checking on her?"

Everyone else Catherine would even consider speaking to had gone to comfort her more than once, so it was definitely my turn. "Of course, aunt."

With everyone outside, the house was eerily quiet. I couldn't even hear Catherine, though she'd run into the house sobbing.

"Cat?" I called, my voice echoing off the tile floors.

I moved through a side door, down a corridor, and into the main entrance hall without seeing or hearing a single sign of my cousin.

"Catherine? Are you all right?" I called. Still, there was no answer.

I'd been debating all morning whether Mr. Matcham's death was the one foretold by the Chess Master or whether I should still be on alert for yet another death in our party. These thoughts only added to the anxiety I felt each time I called for Catherine and she didn't respond. Was my cousin dead? Had I allowed the murderer to commit his horrid deed?

I walked up the stairs, thinking and hoping perhaps she had gone to her bedroom to be alone. Her room was on the opposite end of the hallway from Mr. Matcham's, and I continued calling for her as I made my way to her door and knocked three times.

"Catherine? Are you in here?" I asked. My heart began to beat quickly. Would I open the door and find my cousin the way Dr. Shaw had found Mr. Matcham?

"Catherine?" I called again, gathering all my courage and cracking the door open. "I'm coming inside now."

Her room was dark as I opened the door, and my eyes darted to her bed immediately, half-expecting to see her lying there in a prone position.

Mercifully, the room was empty. It didn't exactly quell my concerns that Catherine had been murdered, but I at least knew she had not been murdered in her bedroom. I planned to close the door and continue looking for her, but just as I turned towards the door, something caught my eye. I couldn't say for sure why the slight bulge in the mattress meant anything to me. The duvet was still rumpled from Catherine sleeping in it the night before and the maid, with everything that had happened that morning, hadn't come up to make the beds, so the lump beneath the mattress was almost imperceptible. Almost.

At the bottom corner of the bed, the mattress lifted slightly, as if something had been hastily shoved beneath it and then forgotten. Under normal circumstances, I would have decided it was none of my business. Because, in truth, whatever Catherine had hiding under her mattress *was* none of my business. In this instance, however, I felt I had a duty to the departed

Mr. Matcham to investigate. I wanted to believe my family members were beyond reproach. Certainly, none of them could be capable of murder. I wanted to believe that, but something inside of me still urged me forward. I had to investigate for my brother Jimmy, if for no other reason. The Chess Master had promised me information, and I needed it desperately.

I took slow, light steps across the floor, afraid they would be heard in the silent house and Catherine would run up, demanding to know why I was snooping through her things. After every step and every squeak of the floorboards, I stopped, ear quirked towards the hallway, and listened. Silence. Another step, another squeak. Stop. Listen. Silence. This pattern repeated for what felt like hours, though surely it was only a few seconds.

When I finally reached the bed, my heart was thumping in my chest. Even though I desperately wanted answers as to how Mr. Matcham had died and who, if anyone, had killed him, I didn't want Catherine to be a murderer. I honestly didn't even want to know anything about her personal life. It was easier to love and respect your family members when you knew only the things they wished for you to know. For instance, no one in the Beckingham family would love me if they knew I was truly Nellie Dennet. Of course, my situation was a little different than something hidden beneath Catherine's bed, but the point remained. People had secrets for a reason, and I wanted Catherine to be the sole keeper of hers. Unfortunately, privacy was a luxury no one could afford at such a time.

I pulled back as little of the duvet as possible. I didn't expect Catherine would notice if her bed was slightly more mussed than it had been when she'd left, but I didn't want to take any chances. Then, I reached my hand beneath the mattress and immediately felt a small wooden box wedged just under the corner. I pulled it out and set it on the bed.

The box was a dark stained wood with a matching lid that slid into etched grooves in the sides. It looked like it could have been an expensive cigar box. Though, why Catherine would have a cigar box was beyond me. I carefully slid the lid open, but it caught at an odd angle in the grooves and refused to open anymore. I closed the box and tried again, pulling it out slowly, but yet again the lid caught. I shimmied the wooden piece from side to side, hoping to wiggle it free, but to no avail. Finally, I closed the lid and then yanked it open with all of my strength. This time it opened fully. Unfortunately, the piece of wood broke free from the box entirely and clattered to the floor creating what, to me, sounded like a deafening racket.

I held my breath, waiting for footsteps to move down the hall or for someone to call out to me, wondering what was taking so long. But there was nothing. In the back of my mind, I still couldn't decide whether this was a comfort. Did no one respond to the noise because no one was in the house to hear it or because the person in the house— Catherine—was no longer in a position to hear anything— dead? I pushed my anxious thoughts away and focused on the task at hand. I'd discover what was in the box and then find out where Catherine had disappeared to. If she was dead, a few minutes spent investigating her room wouldn't change that fact, though it would make me feel incredibly guilty.

Confident no one was coming to immediately apprehend me, I turned my focus to the now open box. The contents of which were: a pair of diamond earrings, a red silk pocket square, and a folded piece of paper. The edges of the paper were worn with either time or repeated handling.

I opened it and at once recognized it as a letter. Some of the ink was smudged with fingerprints and water stains, but it was legible enough.

DEAREST CATHERINE,

I HOPE this letter finds you well. You know how difficult I find it to express myself in writing. And with you, more than anyone, I'd much rather express myself in person. But for you and you alone, I will try my best to say what I feel.

IT HAS BEEN TOO LONG since I've laid eyes on your beautiful face. You have doubtless heard talk of the many scandalous affairs I am taking part in on my travels, but please know they are nothing more than salacious rumors. You are the only woman in my life. The one I think of constantly and wish I never had to part from. I cannot wait until the day we can be together in the open, but until then, I will steal whatever moments I can and cherish them always.

I PLAN to be back in London in three weeks. I would be back sooner, but I have to make a stop in the country. A debt to settle with a doctor in Somerset. You know to whom I'm referring, so I won't sully this letter with his name. Please promise me we'll see one another when I return. I know it is hard for you to get away, but I can't spend a minute longer than necessary separated from you.

·   ·   ·

Loving you always,
  Thomas

I READ through the letter several times, committing every line to memory. Who was Thomas? And which doctor from Somerset had he been referring to? I had never guessed my cousin was involved in a secret love affair, but the real question was, why was it secret at all? I'd heard Lady Ashton press Catherine on more than one occasion to find herself a good man. Why would she keep Thomas a secret? Unless, of course, Thomas was not a good man.

"Rose?" a voice I at once recognized as my aunt's echoed through the house. It sounded very distant, as if she was on the staircase. "Rose, where are you?"

"Upstairs," I answered loudly, scrambling to refold the letter and place it back inside the box.

"Catherine is outside with the rest of the guests," she called. I could imagine her ascending the stairs as I slipped the lid into place. "I grew worried when you didn't return."

"I was looking for Catherine," I yelled back as I practically threw myself across the bed to shove the box beneath the mattress. I moved the blanket back over the corner of the mattress, ran through the door, and closed Catherine's door behind me.

By the time I made it into the hallway, Lady Ashton was at the top of the stairs. She saw me standing in front of Catherine's door, narrowed her eyes slightly, and then smiled. "Catherine went for a walk. Edward found her on the trail through the woods. She is taking Mr. Matcham's death quite hard, poor thing."

"Has he been a family friend long?" I asked.

"You don't remember Mr. Matcham from when you were younger?"

I shook my head. "Not much," I said, hoping this wasn't too suspicious. Thus far, everyone in the Beckingham family had been forgiving when I forgot the names of relatives or family acquaintances, but they would eventually find it suspect if I couldn't remember a single person from my life before India.

She looked at me for a long minute, making my palms sweaty, and then shrugged slightly. "That isn't so surprising, I suppose. Mr. Matcham was in his early twenties when you left, and he travelled often."

"Was the travel for work or...?"

"*Or* is right," Lady Ashton said with a bitter laugh. "The man never worked an honest day in his life. His fortune was the kind that came from excessive gambling and unearned luck. I suppose he wasn't so lucky in the end, though, was he?"

"No, I suppose not," I said, surprised by my aunt's coldness. She was usually the epitome of civility. Or, at the very least, of decorum. It seemed very unlike her to speak ill of anyone, especially the dead.

Suddenly, Lady Ashton's eyes widened, and she looked up at me, horror-stricken. "I'm so sorry, Rose. Forgive me. That was terribly unkind."

"No need to apologize," I said, reaching out to touch her shoulder. "It is only the two of us here, and you are free to speak your mind."

"I trust you, Rose, but some things ought never to be said. Especially when they can reveal so much of someone's heart," she said, placing her hand over her chest. "I pride myself on being a kind woman, but where Thomas

Matcham is concerned, I'm afraid I have a tendency to lose my head."

I would have sworn my heart stopped beating in my chest. My ribs seemed to suck inward, crushing my lungs, and it was a miracle I didn't fall over right there. I dropped my hand from my aunt's shoulder and ran it across my stomach as calmly as possible, trying to encourage my body to inhale. *Thomas Matcham.* Had I not, only minutes before, been reading a love letter from Thomas to Lady Ashton's own daughter? Suddenly, it felt as though my aunt could see the truth of what I knew on my face.

"Are you all right, dear? You look a bit pale," she said.

I nodded quickly. "Oh, yes. I'm fine. I think I'm just a little tired."

"You should lie down. The guests will understand if you are feeling unwell. It has been a big day for everyone. Go rest, and I will explain your absence to the others," she said, her head tilted to the side in motherly concern.

"Thank you, aunt. I won't be long."

"There is no rush, dear," she said.

I felt her watching me as I walked down the hall to my room. When the door closed behind me, I felt like I was able to take my first breath in several minutes.

Mr. Matcham's first name was Thomas and I had found a love letter written to Catherine from a well-travelled, debt-collecting man named Thomas. Could that be a coincidence? If so, it would be one of the largest I'd ever heard of. Was Catherine secretly seeing Mr. Matcham? That would certainly explain how closely she'd stuck with him the day before. However, the letter had looked rather old. Either, their relationship had been secret for a long period of time, perhaps even years, or the letter had been written long ago and the relationship had since fizzled out.

If the relationship was no more, how had Catherine taken that news? She seemed very distraught at Mr. Matcham's passing, but I knew better than anyone how easy it could be to play a part. Could Catherine have killed Mr. Matcham to keep him from moving on? Were her tears really from guilt rather than anguish? Or, perhaps, Lady Ashton had found proof of the couple's relationship. She'd said herself that she lost her head when it came to issues regarding Thomas Matcham. What would she do to protect her daughter from the ruined reputation she would no doubt earn by partnering with Mr. Matcham? And then there was another suspect still. In the letter, Mr. Matcham had made reference to a doctor in Somerset. The relationship between the two men was clearly not a good one. Could that doctor have been the same Dr. Shaw who had discovered and examined the body that morning? Who better to deliver a fatal dose of poison than a doctor?

Suddenly, the excuse I'd made to Lady Ashton about feeling tired was no longer a lie. I sat on the edge of my bed and ran my hand across my face. I really would need a nap if I was going to solve this murder, because it was a murder, wasn't it? I'd had my doubts, but the proof continued to stack up. Mr. Matcham had been a healthy young man yesterday, and now he was dead. I now realized it was time to face the facts. The murder the Chess Master had alluded to had occurred, and if I wanted any information on Jimmy or to sleep soundly amongst my family members ever again, I had to solve it.

Mrs. Worthing had been joking before, but her words suddenly rang true. The resident detective was present and ready to solve another murder case.

11

When I rejoined the group, everyone, Lady Harwood included, was still outside. They seemed to prefer the outdoors, especially now that a man had been murdered inside the house, and I couldn't blame them in the least. Catherine still looked puffy and moments away from tears, but she had pulled herself together enough to sit and watch while her siblings and the Barry siblings played a game of croquet in the grass. I suspected it had been my aunt's idea to keep the young people distracted, so there was less time to dwell on the unhappy event that was never far from our minds. Alice and Vivian were beating Edward and Charles, but the men seemed to be letting the women win, which I thought was oddly charitable of Edward.

Despite the somber cloud hanging over the party, the weather was quite lovely. Sunshine flecked through the overhang of trees, creating bright spots in the grass, and a cool breeze rolled across the grounds constantly, acting as nature's fan. It was a picturesque afternoon. Vivian and

Charles sported matching brown flannel outfits, and Alice's yellow dress had a smart, crisp white collar. Edward, per usual, wore a dark suit. He looked as ready for an office as the garden.

Out of the whole party, only Lady Harwood seemed to mind the breeze. She frowned and pulled her shawl tightly around her shoulders to combat the light gust.

"Are you feeling better, Rose?" Lady Ashton asked as I approached.

Lord Ashton, Catherine, Mr. and Mrs. Worthing, Lady Harwood, and Dr. Shaw all turned at the mention of my name to watch me approach their chosen spot in the shade.

"Yes, a nap can do wonders," I said with a smile.

This pleased Lady Ashton, and everyone turned back to the game, except for Dr. Shaw. I couldn't help but notice his gaze lingered on me much longer than everyone else's. I offered him a wide smile, but his eyebrows still pulled together, and he only looked away when Lady Harwood complained about a horrible cramp in her calf.

"If I'm alive tomorrow it will be a miracle," she said, looking up at the sky and shaking her head.

"You are perfectly healthy, Lady Harwood." Dr. Shaw spoke the words with familiarity, as though he had repeated them one hundred times before. And with Lady Harwood, it wouldn't surprise me if he had.

"We thought Mr. Matcham was perfectly healthy, as well. Didn't we?" she argued, lip curled. "Whatever is going around, it will come for me next. The young and the elderly can't withstand such things."

Dr. Shaw took a deep breath but otherwise remained remarkably unflapped. "Mr. Matcham was neither young nor old, Lady Harwood."

"My point exactly," the old woman said. "If a man in his prime can die of this mysterious illness, then an old woman has no chance. You ought to begin looking for new employment, Dr. Shaw."

"Lady Harwood, we have no reason to believe Mr. Matcham died from any kind of illness," Lady Ashton said, trying to intervene.

"It could have been any of thousands of different causes," Mrs. Worthing added.

Lady Harwood let out an exaggerated cough and looked at the two women. "Unknown illness could have been one of those thousands of causes. By all means, deny it if that is a comfort to you. I, on the other hand, like to be realistic. And the reality here is that I am the next most likely person amongst us to fall."

"If you are so concerned about this illness, why not go home?" Lord Ashton asked, clearly much less patient than everyone else. Lady Ashton gave her husband a reproachful glance, though I sensed a bit of amusement in it. The woman's dronings about death and dying were making everyone a little weary.

Lady Harwood didn't seem to mind. She simply laughed at Lord Ashton as if he were the most foolish man she'd ever met. "And sully my own home with the disease? No thank you. I'd much rather remain here and wait it out. If by some miracle I do not fall ill and die in the night, then I will return home comforted that I won't take anything nasty back with me."

Lord Ashton mumbled something under his breath about Lady Harwood and nastiness, but I couldn't hear him, and I suspected Lady Harwood couldn't either. Lady Ashton bit back a smile and shook her head at her husband.

Catherine, while no longer sobbing, remained completely silent. She sat on a low stone wall around one of the gardens, her hand folded under her chin, her navy-blue tea dress fluttering around her calves in the wind, looking like a morose woman from a Victorian painting. I observed my cousin's innate beauty—even after hours of crying she still looked striking—and wondered what she could have seen in a man like Thomas Matcham. He was handsome enough, but he reminded me too much of an oil spill beneath a car to be tempting. He wore his black hair slicked back to his head, so everyone knew the intimate shape of his skull. His face had the sweaty pallor of someone on the verge of a fever. He had redeeming qualities, but again, they were hidden behind a layer of sheen. Whereas, Catherine was bright, vibrant. Bouncing golden hair, luminescent skin, clear blue eyes. I tried to imagine them meeting secretly, and all I could think was that the sun and the moon never shared the same space in the sky. Their relationship confounded me to the point that I wondered whether another Thomas couldn't have written the letter. But that, of course, was only wishful thinking.

By the time the game of croquet was winding down and the players came back to rejoin the group—Vivian smiling broadly at Edward, teasing him about the victory, though Edward didn't seem as amused—Lady Harwood was ready to go inside.

"This breeze is seconds away from blowing me away, Dr. Shaw," she complained with a scowl.

Had I been a less kind person, I would have pointed out that Lady Harwood, being a rather stout woman, was in no danger of blowing away in any kind of wind, especially such a light one, but I bit my tongue.

"Would you like to return to the Hall?" Dr. Shaw asked,

already standing up in anticipation of the woman's response.

"Yes, I think I would."

By the time Dr. Shaw tucked Lady Harwood's legs up into her wheelchair, repositioned her shawl several times, and pulled her out of the deep ruts her wheels had caused in the soft grass of the garden, he was the one in danger of being blown away. He looked white as a sheet and sweaty.

"That poor man," Mrs. Worthing said to me as the old woman and her doctor disappeared inside. "Surely, he could find work with another less demanding patient."

I said, "But what kind of reputation would he have as a personal physician if word got around that he traded in an old woman because she was too much work."

Mrs. Worthing shrugged and nodded in agreement. "But still, better to find a new profession altogether than spend your days like that."

Everyone was talking animatedly about the croquet game and Charles was doing his best to try and lure Catherine into playing. She responded with a hard shake of her head and then marched off towards the tree line.

"I'm sorry," he said to no one in particular, his face brimming with disappointment. "I didn't mean to upset her."

"She's feeling out of sorts today, Charles," Lady Ashton said, patting the sad man on the shoulder. "Lord Ashton, perhaps you should accompany your daughter on her walk."

Lord Ashton grumbled as he crossed the lawn, taking high steps to avoid the swampy parts of the grass, but he still did as his wife asked.

"I suppose we are all a little out of sorts," Charles admitted.

"I don't see why. It's a beautiful day," Edward said with an uncharacteristic amount of cheer.

"A man has died," Mr. Worthing said, speaking up for the first time in a while. While on the ship from Bombay to London, it was rare to find Mr. Worthing not engaged in some trivial conversation about something or other, but he had been rather quiet all morning. Mr. Matcham's death apparently had him out of sorts, as well.

"Of course," Edward said, sobering. "I just meant, *aside from that* it is a beautiful day."

Mr. Worthing opened his mouth, clearly preparing to argue, but Lady Ashton, ever the peacemaker, stepped in. "Edward is a man of practicalities, Mr. Worthing. You'll have to excuse him. Emotions have little part to play in his thinking."

This seemed to settle Mr. Worthing, and Edward gave his mother a small smile in appreciation which she didn't return.

I was paying attention to the conversation, but in the midst of it, I'd noticed something out of the corner of my eye. A black leather bag with stiff, square handles resting against the stairs from the terrace down into the garden. Dr. Shaw's medical bag. In all of the adjusting he had to do with Lady Harwood before she was ready to head back inside, it was no wonder he had forgotten it. Inside, I knew he kept Lady Harwood's medications along with all of his instruments—stethoscope, thermometer, and more—which Lady Harwood required once an hour to feel confident she wasn't on the verge of death. So, he would no doubt be back for it soon. Which meant I had to work quickly.

The "insect bite" on Mr. Matcham's arm would not leave my mind. The idea that a perfectly healthy man could die in the night and have a single, perfectly-circular insect bite on the inside of his arm seemed a bit too coincidental to me. So, if it was like I thought and he had been poisoned, where better to find the poison than the doctor's medical bag? No one looked in it aside from Dr. Shaw and, the current moment aside, he kept it with him always. It would be the perfect place to hide the evidence, and now was my opportunity to investigate.

"Oh," I said suddenly, drawing the attention of the group. "Dr. Shaw left his medical bag out here."

"Someone should run it up to him," Vivian said. She placed a hand on her brother's shoulder. "Charles, perhaps you ought to."

Charles made a move towards the bag, but I jumped up and grabbed it, holding it with both hands in front of me, the weight of it pressing back against my knee caps. "Oh no, I am happy to do it."

"It looks quite heavy," Vivian said with a frown.

I smiled at her and shook my head. "It's no trouble. I'd be happy to."

She opened her mouth to say something, but I was already up the stairs and crossing the terrace towards the house. I knew I could go through the main set of doors and be in the entrance hall directly outside of the corridor where Dr. Shaw and Lady Harwood were, but I didn't want to chance Dr. Shaw seeing me before I wanted him to. So, I casually angled myself towards a side door, which led into the kitchen.

If anyone in the garden noticed my strange decision to enter through the kitchen, they said nothing and after waiting several seconds, I felt content none of the guests had followed me.

But that did not mean I was alone. Hearing the voices of approaching servants, most likely the cook and a helper, I looked around for a hiding place. I saw an open doorway off the kitchen and dodged into a little nook filled with shiny cupboards. I assumed it was a butler's pantry or something of the sort. After a moment, the voices passed by and I sighed with relief.

Vivian was right, Dr. Shaw's bag weighed at least twenty pounds, and it took a good deal of strength to lift it by the handles onto the top of the small table before me. Once it was there, I paused and took a deep breath to settle my nerves. Then, I flicked open the golden clasp and let gravity pull the bag open.

As I already knew, the bag was full of medications for Lady Harwood and a slew of medical instruments. Some I recognized and some I'd never seen before. What I hadn't expected was how similar everything would look. For some reason, I'd half-expected to open the bag and see a section devoted to Lady Harwood and then a dark corner of the bag labeled "poisons" or "For Mr. Matcham." Of course, this was not the case.

I set to work sorting through the bag. I could skip over all the pills, as they could not have been injected into Mr. Matcham's arm. I was searching for a syringe or a vial of liquid. Preferably, both. I placed the pill bottles in a line along the countertop, so I would know in what order to return them to the bag to keep Dr. Shaw from being suspicious, and I placed the different shiny silver medical instruments in a pile in front of them. As I neared the bottom of the bag, I knew I would find what I'd been looking for. It had to be Dr. Shaw. He had the experience to inject a poison and would know how large of a dose to give someone of Mr. Matcham's size. Not to mention, he had discovered the man's body and done the initial examination. What kind of evidence had he tampered with in those critical moments?

However, when the bottom of the bag came into view, all that remained inside was a white handkerchief and a few clean rags. Once I removed those, the bag was empty. Fruitlessly, I searched for a hidden pocket or compartment. I even went so far as to tip the bag upside down and shake it furiously, but nothing fell out. As much as I didn't want Dr. Shaw to be a murderer, I still felt disappointed. Even though I'd found the love letter from Mr. Matcham in Catherine's possession, Dr. Shaw had still been my strongest suspect. It made the most sense that a man who built his career on preserving life would also be capable of taking it. Now, though, I had no proof at all to back that theory up. Dejected, I placed the items back inside the bag just as I'd found them. First, the rags and handkerchief. Then, the instruments in a small pile on the right, and finally the pills. I nestled them into the folds of the rags to help them stay upright, and I was dropping the last bottle into the bag when the door to the pantry squeaked open.

"What do you think you are doing?"

With my hand still inside the bag, I looked up into the angry eyes of Dr. Shaw. He must have seen me duck into the pantry with his bag and now he stood in the doorway looking down on me, his face flaming red.

"What are you doing in my bag?" he demanded.

I removed my hand and stepped back, placing more distance between us. Although I hadn't found proof that he was a murderer, he looked angry enough to kill just then, and I didn't want to be within arm's reach of him.

"You left your bag outside," I said. This was true but didn't explain why I had been elbow deep inside of it.

"Then how did it find its way in here and why were you rooting through it?" he asked, yanking the bag across the table with enough force that I heard its contents rattling and tipping over.

My mouth opened and closed uselessly. I tried to think of a good explanation, but I hadn't anticipated being captured, so I had nothing prepared.

Dr. Shaw shifted through the bag, doing a kind of mental calculation of what might be missing. "Are you trying to make me look guilty?" he snapped.

"What?" I asked, not understanding the question.

"You seemed insistent earlier that Mr. Matcham was murdered by poison. When you asked for my opinion on the matter, I hoped that would be the end of things. But now, I find you rooting through my bag."

"I can explain," I began.

"So it seems," he continued, speaking over me, his voice booming off of the tile floors, "like you are trying to point the finger at the doctor. The man who always carries medications and syringes and all the equipment necessary to inject someone with a deadly poison."

"Dr. Shaw, I assure you—"

"I will not go down so easily, Miss Beckingham. Let me assure you of that fact at once. You can plant whatever you'd like in my bag, but I have lived in this part of the world for a long time. I have more friends and connections than you could ever dream of. Making me out to be a killer is going to require much more than dropping something suspicious into my bag."

"Check the bag," I insisted. "You'll see there is nothing in there."

"Because I caught you just in time," he said, lip curled back. "I've heard the rumors that swirl about me. The stories that claim I lost my inheritance to a gambling habit, and much of it went to Mr. Matcham. But you'd be hard pressed to find any proof of that, and I gain nothing from Mr. Matcham's death, regardless. So, I suggest you point the finger at someone else before I cut it off."

With a final huff, Dr. Shaw snapped the clasp closed, grabbed his bag, and stormed out of the pantry, the wooden door swinging behind him.

I TOOK several minutes to compose myself, and then slipped out of the pantry, walked back through the door onto the terrace and moved towards where everyone had been gathered in the garden. Now, I could see the majority of the group tromping through the thick grass in the direction of the tree line. Only Edward and Lady Ashton remained near the stairs. Lady Ashton signaled for Edward, and he crossed the short space between them and then leaned down at his mother's urging. She appeared to be whispering something in his ear, and I tried to approach quietly to maybe catch a bit of what it was. However, my shoe scuffed on the uneven stones of the terrace and Lady Ashton's head snapped up. In a second, she was smiling up at me.

"Rose, dear, did you find Dr. Shaw?" she asked, patting the spot next to her for me to sit down.

"I did." I hoped my face did not betray the altercation we'd just had in the kitchen.

As I neared them, I noticed Edward looked puzzled. His dark brows were pulled together and he wouldn't take his narrowed eyes off of his mother. She, on the other hand, refused to look at him.

Clearly, I'd stumbled into something. Or rather, interrupted something. What had Lady Ashton been preparing to whisper in Edward's ear? I focused on the thought only until I heard my name echoing across the garden.

Alice was calling for me to follow her, and happy to forget my investigation if for only a few minutes, I did so happily.

12

I was glad to think of anything other than the murder of Thomas Matcham for a few hours, but by dinner, it was the only thought in my head, and frustration had begun to take hold. I had scraps of information, tiny pieces of a larger puzzle, and I knew I only needed to arrange them in the right way to see the full picture, but it felt impossible. Catherine had a love letter, Lady Ashton had a dislike of Mr. Matcham, Mr. Matcham had a bad reputation and an insect bite, and Dr. Shaw had poverty brought on by gambling debts and a great knowledge of poison. None of these pieces of information, individually, led to murder. But together? I still wasn't sure.

On the ship and back in London, when I'd stumbled upon murder investigations, I'd had the luxury of time. Now, however, all of the guests at Ridgewick Hall, myself included, had one more full day at the estate before everyone would go their separate ways. That gave me just over thirty-six hours to solve the case and apprehend a suspect, or else... Well, I wasn't sure. If I solved the case, the Chess Master promised me information about my brother Jimmy, which would be quite welcome. There had been no information about what would happen if I should fail to solve the case. The Chess Master knew my secret. He knew I was not truly Rose Beckingham, so perhaps the punishment would be the reveal of my deception. He would tell the people I had come to regard as family about how I had lied to them and stolen the inheritance that would have passed to them. I would certainly be arrested, unless I managed to escape. But even then, would I live my life on the run? Take on yet another identity and hide like a rat in the cover of night for the remainder of my life?

I could feel myself beginning to unravel, so I stopped in front of the full-length mirror in my room, placed my hand on my chest, and monitored my breathing until it returned to normal. I had to stay calm and think clearly, otherwise I would never solve the case. Thirty-six hours was not a long amount of time, but it was better than nothing. I would just have to do my best. After separating in various directions throughout the estate, everyone would be together again for dinner and for drinks afterward in the drawing room. I would have to use the time wisely. Observe everyone and look for any signs of deception, which, considering the level of my own deception, I should be able to spot quite easily.

The satin of my emerald green dress brushed against my skin like water and floated down to the floor. It was a fine garment, probably too fine for the evening ahead, but it gave me a kind of confidence I needed.

The assembled guests were much less lively than earlier in the day. Everyone seemed content to eat and let Mrs. Worthing and Vivian carry the conversation, each of them working to lure Mr. Worthing and Edward, respectively, into the discussion, as well. However, neither of the men seemed interested in the latest women's fashions of London or in how things differed in the States.

"We get everything first, of course," Vivian said with an air of snobbery. "By the time it reaches the women there, it is watered down, and we have moved on to something better."

Even though the better part of my life had been spent in India, and I now claimed myself to be a Londoner, I had a strong desire to defend my countrywomen. However, I held my tongue, deciding this was not an important enough issue to raise any suspicion about my loyalties.

"No one can wear fashion like we London women can," Mrs. Worthing said with a cheeky giggle. She winked at me and then gave Catherine a smile, though Catherine didn't return it.

The dinner carried on that way. Dr. Shaw spoke only to Lady Harwood, who was still insistent upon her upcoming demise, and looked at me three times throughout the meal, each time to level me with a menacing glare. Everyone else simply ate their food and stood to leave when the meal was finished. I could not have been more disappointed. I'd hoped for some piece of information to come to light that would help my investigation. Anything, really. But instead, I'd only learned about Vivian's favorite hat shops in town and where Mrs. Worthing bought her shoes.

My shoulders slumped forward as I left the dining room and headed for the sitting room. I was the last one to leave, and a servant was already beginning to gather the plates. Consumed with thoughts of my impending failure and the fallout that would likely occur because of it, I almost didn't notice the hushed voices coming from the hallway between the sitting room and the servant's corridor. Almost.

The voices caught my attention and I stopped moving at

once, quirking my head to the side and then taking soft, slow footsteps towards the edge of the open door. Through the smallest crack in the wooden door, I could see Lady Ashton and Edward standing in the dark, no more than a few inches away from one another.

"I hoped to talk to you earlier," Edward whispered. "Father said you collected a few of Mr. Matcham's things to send back to his family, and I'd like to take a look at them."

"Why would you need to look through his things?" she asked. "Of what importance are a dead man's belongings to you?"

"I am not after his belongings. I'm after my money," he said.

"Your money? As I recall, he won it from you fairly."

Edward snorted. "Even if that were true, he has no need for it now, and I would like to take it back."

"It is unethical, and I will not be party to it," Lady Ashton said, crossing her arms and shaking her head.

"His family doesn't even know about the money. They will not miss it. I am the only person alive who will miss it, in fact. It seems unethical to keep it from me, considering I am the only one who will suffer because of its absence."

"You are not near as convincing as you think you are, son," Lady Ashton said with a surprising amount of animosity. "And I will not allow it, so do not bother asking again."

"I was being courteous by asking," Edward said.

Lady Ashton's eyes narrowed. "Are you threatening to break into my room?"

"Only if you refuse me access. I'm sorry to do this, but—"

"Where is the son I once knew?" Lady Ashton asked. "What has become of my kind boy? I do not recognize the man who stands before me."

"Do not be so dramatic, Mother. I assume you did not count the money, and therefore won't be able to recognize if a chunk of it is missing. I won't tell you if I've done the deed, and you can proceed with the belief that I left the money alone. Then, everyone is happy."

Lady Ashton's fists clenched at her side and she appeared to be shaking. "Do not presume to understand me so easily. You know nothing of what I am protecting you from. Sneak into my room and you may find more than you bargained for. So, I'd urge you to leave well enough alone."

I wanted to stay and listen to more of the conversation, but I also sensed it was coming to a close, and I didn't want to be caught listening outside the door. As quickly and quietly as possible, I backed away from the door, slipped back into the dining room, and then crossed into the entrance hall. Once there, I took the stairs to the next floor and found myself standing outside the largest bedroom. The room belonging to Lady Ashton.

The decision to look through Lady Ashton's things had come to me the moment I'd heard she had some of Mr. Matcham's belongings. However, the urge grew even stronger when I saw how viscerally she reacted to the idea of her son looking through her things. *You may find more than you bargained for.*

The door was unlocked, so before I could second guess my decision, I was inside and closing the door softly behind me. The sitting room was on the opposite end of the house, so even if my footsteps echoed upstairs, no one would pay them any mind. The only thing I had to worry myself with was being gone too long. Dr. Shaw had made it clear that morning that he had noticed my absences from the group, and I didn't want to give him any reason to point this out to the rest of the party.

A four-poster bed sat in the middle of the room, blue velvet curtains hanging from each corner. To the right was a large armoire and a set of drawers next to that, but I was more focused on the trunk at the end of the bed. The trunk Lady Ashton had arrived with the day before. The same trunk she would return to London with. And the trunk she had, no doubt, stored away anything of Mr. Matcham's that she intended to send to his family.

I knelt down in front of the trunk, moving my dress out of the way so I didn't wrinkle the delicate fabric, and lifted the metal clasp. It made a metallic clank against the top of the trunk, which sounded deafening in the quiet room. I paused, expecting someone to barge into the room and catch me red-handed the way Dr. Shaw had in the pantry that morning. However, no one came. So, I lifted the trunk lid, cursing the creaky hinge the entire way, until it rested against the footboard of the bed. Then, I began to snoop.

No matter how many times I looked through people's private belongings, it never became easier. I never felt comfortable doing it. There could be an argument made that it was all for the greater good, but it was a flimsy argument even to my own ears. I was invading the privacy of someone I loved and trusted, and I wanted to be done with it as soon as possible.

A maid must have unpacked most of Lady Ashton's clothes, but her shoes and a number of hats were still organized in the bottom of the trunk. Then, in the front corner was a small stash of items wrapped up in a handkerchief. It looked far too simple to belong to either my aunt or my uncle, so I concluded it must have been Mr. Matcham's and pulled it out.

The four corners were tied into a knot, and when I undid it, the contents inside spilled out. There was a small stack of pocket squares similar to the one I'd seen inside the box in Catherine's room—further cementing the fact that her Thomas had been none other than Thomas Matcham—a money clip filled with cash, and a separate billfold. I picked up the billfold to examine it and by sheer luck, it slipped from my hands and knocked over the stack of pocket squares. As the pocket squares slid out of their stack, a small piece of metal became visible. It looked like the pin on the back of a brooch. I reached for it, and then dropped it again with a gasp.

Folded between Mr. Matcham's pocket squares was a small syringe. I wouldn't have noticed it had the stack not toppled sideways. The glass cylinder at the center was still damp with some unknown liquid, proving that the syringe had been used somewhat recently.

Immediately, I began returning the items to the handkerchief. I tied the knot and dropped it all right back where I found it. Then, I hurried into the hallway and away from my aunt's door.

My mind was reeling. I had no idea what to expect when I'd walked into that room and opened the trunk. Lady Ashton had told Edward that he might find more than he bargained for if he went snooping around her room, and it had seemed suspicious, but I had never really expected to find what I believed to be the murder weapon. But I had. And now I had to decide what to do with that information. And what it meant.

Just because Lady Ashton had the syringe didn't mean she was the killer. She could have found the syringe in Mr. Matcham's room and hid it to keep anyone from knowing his death had been a suicide. However, I found that hard to believe. Mr. Matcham had just won a good deal of money at cards and, if the letter in Catherine's box had any bearing on their current relationship, he had the affections of a beautiful young woman. Plus, with so much concern about a possible murder or a mysterious illness, wouldn't Lady Ashton have wanted to calm her guests' fears?

As I moved down the stairs and closer to the sitting room where I would come face to face with my aunt, I positioned the puzzle pieces I'd found into the full picture.

Lady Ashton, in fear for her daughter's reputation and the Beckingham family name, had poisoned Thomas Matcham in his sleep to separate him from Catherine. My aunt, Lady Ashton, was a murderer.

13

J ust as had been the case with dinner, the post-meal gathering in the sitting room was rather subdued. Everyone was quiet and tired, so the party, thankfully, broke up rather early, everyone taking to their respective rooms for the night. I spoke to Lady Ashton only once when she wished me goodnight while standing in the doorway of her room, where I had so recently been snooping. I smiled, incapable of forming words, and gratefully ducked into my own room for the night.

Sleep, once again, did not come easily. The night before it had been due to my concerns over who, if anyone in the party, would be murdered. Now, my thoughts were focused on my aunt. She was the murderer. I was almost sure of it. But what could I do with that information?

In order to receive the reward the Chess Master had promised, I had to turn her in, but could I really do that? While what Lady Ashton had done was wrong—there was never an excuse for murder—she had done it out of love for her daughter. She was not a crazed murderer and I had no reason to believe she would ever strike again. Moreover, the

Beckinghams were the closest thing I had to family. If I ostracized myself from them, I would be almost entirely alone in the world.

But then, if I didn't tell, there was a chance I would lose the Beckinghams anyway when the Chess Master told them about my true identity and I would miss out on receiving the reward I'd been promised. Without information on Jimmy or the financial means to continue employing Achilles Prideaux, I wouldn't have a chance of finding my brother. Then, I really would be all alone in the world.

When morning finally came, I felt half-alive. Exhaustion stung my eyes and the face that met me in the mirror was pallid and stretched.

Breakfast revived me only slightly. Lady Ashton asked me several times if I was feeling all right—this was fodder enough for Lady Harwood to insist I'd come down with the same illness as Mr. Matcham—and I did my best to assure her I was fine without making direct eye contact. My exhaustion served to make my emotions seem more unmanageable, and I worried I'd burst into tears if my eyes met those of my aunt.

"Gentlemen," Lord Ashton boomed, standing from the table so abruptly that his chair nearly tipped over behind him. "I've planned something special for today. I believe it's a beautiful day for pheasant hunting."

There was an enthusiastic response from the men around the table. I suspected this was an activity my uncle must have planned in haste, probably at my aunt's urging, to distract everyone from our unpleasant circumstances.

There was a brief wait after the meal, as everyone went upstairs to dress appropriately for the hunt, and then we all moved outdoors. Though I and the other ladies would only be participating as observers, I was glad to be out in the sunshine, where I had room to move and think without so many sets of eyes on me.

Our party was packed into several waiting cars and then made a short journey across the estate. We stopped and clambered out near a large field edged by a stand of trees, where we found servants in wool coats and flat caps had assembled bearing guns and ammunition for the gentlemen. As I understood it, pheasants would be hiding in the tall grass of the near field, waiting to be frightened into flight by beaters driving them into the air for easier shooting.

I had no desire to view the event up close and when the actual hunting began, the persistent ringing of the gunshots made my already frazzled nerves even more unbearable.

"I'm going for a walk," I said to the small group of onlookers who had settled beneath a large shady tree.

"Would you like any company?" Lady Ashton asked, beginning to rise.

"No, thank you," I said. "It will only be a quick jaunt. I'll be back in a few minutes."

She seemed disappointed but waved me on. Then, when I'd moved several more yards away, she called out to me again. "Mind you don't venture too far south, Rose. The men will be shooting in that direction. Stay behind the large willow on the corner there and you will be safe."

I nodded in thanks and rushed off towards the tree line. How could someone so kind, so motherly, be a murderer? If I'd learned anything in the months since the car explosion in Simla, it was that anyone was capable of murder. Life could rarely be anticipated, and I had been on the receiving end of that lesson too many times to count. The unexpected happened every day. But still, my mind struggled to wrap around the truth of it.

The overgrown path grew denser the deeper I walked but weaving my way through the overgrown vines and branches felt a little like moving through the untamed maze of my own thoughts. I hoped that by the time I made it back to the Beckinghams and their guests, my mind would be decided on how best to proceed with the information I had about Lady Ashton.

I felt I had two options: keep the information to myself and wait to see how the Chess Master chose to respond or tell the entire group what I'd found in Lady Ashton's trunk and alert the police. Neither option felt like a winner, but that was why I'd gone on the walk.

I stepped over a tree root which had grown into the path and threatened to trip me if I wasn't careful, and then pushed a thick branch out of my way, revealing a person in the path.

I startled before realizing it was a member from my own party.

"Edward," I said with a small laugh. "You startled me."

As I was speaking, Edward turned and I noticed the hole he had been digging in the dirt. Then, I noticed the gun his father had given him only a few minutes before. His hand choked up on the handle, his finger tapping dangerously close to the trigger.

"Rose," he said, his voice stretched tight, moments from snapping.

I took a step backward, my survival instincts kicking in before my brain could catch up. "I was out for a walk. I must have gone further than I intended."

I looked ahead and could just barely see the willow tree Lady Ashton had pointed out. It was still a good deal farther north. I hadn't ventured out of bounds. Edward had. But why?

"I'll just turn back and get out of your way," I said, beginning to turn. Before I could, though, Edward raised his gun and leveled it at my chest.

"You'd better stay where you are, Rose."

"Edward don't be daft," I said, still trying to joke. "Don't point that thing at me."

He shook his head, looking genuinely disappointed. "Once again, you've somehow stumbled too close to the truth, and unfortunately, I can't afford for this truth to come to light."

"You aren't making any sense," I said. Though, deep down, I knew he made perfect sense. The puzzle pieces I'd arranged in my mind slid apart and began to create a different picture.

"Don't move, cousin. Please don't make this harder than it has to be," he said, closing one eye and aiming the long gun directly at my heart.

In my mind's eye, the image of my aunt slipping the needle into Mr. Matcham's sleeping arm changed slightly. Rather than her petite frame standing next to the gambler's bed, I saw a head of dark hair and a black suit. I saw my cousin delivering the fatal poison. Lady Ashton didn't kill Mr. Matcham. Edward did. And now, he planned to kill me, too.

14

"You didn't, Edward," I said, closing my eyes and shaking my head. "You didn't do it. Tell me you didn't."

The idea of my aunt being a murderer had been hard to take, but without any direct confirmation from her, I'd been able to hold onto the small hope that perhaps she hadn't actually done it. Perhaps there was another explanation. But now, with Edward's gun pointed at my heart, he was as good as confessing. There could be no doubt. He'd done it, and something inside of me broke. Whether it was exhaustion or emotional fatigue or a mix of the two, tears began to spill down my cheeks and I didn't even have the strength to lift my arm and wipe them away.

"I'm sorry, Rose." His words were apologetic, but there was a flatness to his voice that gave me chills.

"But I saw the syringe in your mother's trunk," I said, still trying to make sense of the sudden turn of events.

"You never could keep your nose in your own business," Edward said in a surprisingly playful tone, considering the circumstances. "My mother must have found the syringe amongst my belongings and tried to hide it. She feared what would become of me if anyone else were to discover the truth, which is why I'm afraid I won't be able to let you leave these woods."

"Why did you kill him?" I asked. I had to know. Needed to know. If, after everything I'd been through, I was going to die in the woods at the hands of someone who believed himself to be my cousin, I deserved to know why.

"For Catherine." He lifted his chin and straightened his shoulders. "And for our family."

"You knew about the love affair?" I asked, the words from Mr. Matcham's letter to Catherine filling my mind. He had claimed to love Catherine and only Catherine very deeply.

Edward laughed, though it sounded more like a cough. "Calling it an affair is an exaggeration. It was a dalliance and nothing more. Mr. Matcham was well known for his long line of flings. The poor women he left in his wake suffered destroyed reputations and fractured family connections. He ruined them, and Catherine would have been no different."

"I saw a letter he wrote to her," I admitted, deciding the time for secrets had long passed. "He seemed to care for her."

"He seemed to, didn't he?" Edward asked, looking away from me and up into the trees for a moment, thoughtful. "He was a good actor, I'll give him that. He had been leading her on for the better part of a year. Encouraging her interest with well-timed attention. While in town, he'd see her once or twice. While travelling, he'd write her a letter every few weeks. It was just enough to keep her interested, but not enough to cut into his many other similar relationships, I'm sure. He played her for a fool."

"Do you know that for a fact?" I asked.

"I know men," he snapped at me, his teeth bared. "And I knew Matcham. Rotten man. Rotten life. I did the world a favor."

I stepped away from him, nervous he would pull the trigger prematurely in his anger. "If you believed he didn't really care for Catherine, why not ask him to leave her?"

"Do you believe murder was my first choice?" he asked.

I wanted to tell him that up until a few seconds before, I wouldn't have believed murder would ever have been an option for him.

"I asked Mr. Matcham to leave my sister alone," he said. "I offered him a good sum of money to do so. He refused."

"Was that not a sign of his true affections, then? Mr. Matcham seemed like a man who cared a good deal for riches. If Catherine meant more to him than money, surely that meant something to you?"

"It was a sign of his power. Matcham was always looking for ways to climb the ladder, to rise into the higher social classes, even as he despised those above him and liked to cause us embarrassment. And my anger only served to increase his enjoyment," Edward said, his face turning red just from the memory. "In the end, murder was my only option."

"So, you decided to poison him while he was a guest at your family estate? Doesn't that seem a little suspicious? Weren't you afraid someone would figure it out?" I asked, trying to understand Edward's line of thinking.

"It was the only place I've ever been seen socially with Thomas Matcham. It would have been far more suspicious for me to meet with him for the first time in London and then have him drop dead a few hours later. Here, he has been a guest of my family several times and invited many more times, though he often refused. This time, however, I was sure to include in the invitation that Catherine would be here, as well. She was a prize he couldn't refuse. So, I lured him here, snuck into his room while he slept, and injected him with the poison. I took a chance that the mark from the injection would not be noticed by the authorities."

"And that's what you are burying now?" I asked, looking in the hole along the side of the trail. "The vial holding the remains of the fatal dose?"

He nodded. "For help with that, I contacted a large presence from London's criminal underworld. Someone most people would be happy to know nothing about. He helps people deal with problems similar to mine. He gave me a rare poison, unheard of in most of the world, that goes undetected by medical professionals and mimics a heart attack. For a price, of course. Unfortunately, because of a few mistakes in my past, I already owed this man a great deal of money. Asking for this second favor only indebted me further. That should be punishment enough. I will never escape my debts to this man."

Edward seemed to be rambling, relieved to be unburdening himself of the secret. His voice was rising in pitch and volume, and his eyes darted around wildly. It was obvious to me that he was nearing a state of hysteria.

"I understand what it means to be desperate," I said, hoping to bring him back to himself. "I can understand how you must have felt."

He looked at me as though he were seeing through me. "How could you understand? Are you referring to the death of your parents? Because, as I recall it, you received a notable sum of money that has softened that blow."

If Edward hadn't been pointing a gun at me, I would have slapped him. How could money ever make up for the lives of people I'd cared about? "They were your aunt and uncle. Surely, that means something to you."

"They abandoned our family for India. We scarcely heard a word from them until news of their deaths arrived. Forgive me if I wasn't heartbroken at the news," he said.

"What of me?" I asked, hoping to touch on a bit of mercy. "Am I worth nothing to you?"

"You, dear cousin, are worth a great deal to me, in fact," he said. "As I believe you already know, we were informed of your death before you arrived to live with us in London, and I was to inherit a large sum of money. It would be enough to set up my life in London and begin to pay off my debts."

"Do you only think of money?"

"That is easy to say when you have plenty of it," Edward shouted, waving the gun at me. "You have never been desperate the way I am."

"Surely your father--"

"I could never tell my father of my debts or ask him for help. His own finances are uneasy enough. Not that I would expect you to understand that."

I wanted to tell Edward of my childhood in New York. Of sleeping on the floor and eating lukewarm broth to survive. But I couldn't do any of that without revealing my true identity, which would be reason enough for him to shoot me on the spot. The inheritance he talked about would have truly been his family's had I not deceived everyone into believing I was Rose Beckingham. But still, if I was careful not to reveal too much, I thought I could tell him a few details of my own story. Enough for him to see he was not alone in the world.

"Someone I loved very dearly found themselves in a situation similar to yours," I said, talking soft and slow, hoping to lull Edward into a calmer state. "He was accused of a horrible crime I do not believe he committed, and the entire world turned on him. He ran away, leaving only a secret message scribbled on a bit of paper, and has not been seen since."

"What did the message say?" Edward asked, his eyes more curious than murderous now.

I reached into the front of my dress and pulled out my golden locket, flicking it open in the palm of my hand. The small scrap of paper rolled out and I unfolded it.

"*Help me*," I read, holding the note out for him to see. "It was discovered at a crime scene, and I believe it was intended for me. I believe he wanted me to find him and help him prove his innocence. So, that is what I am seeking to do. It is why I came back to London. It is why I carry this locket around my neck always. I am doing my best to, as your mother tried to do for you, find this person and protect them from the judgment of the world."

Edward nodded solemnly, soaking in the story I'd relayed for him, and then he released a labored sigh. "So, because of your unnamed friend, you understand my circumstances. You know that I must protect myself from the judgment of the world. You understand that I can't let you leave."

My mouth fell open and I shook my head. "No, Edward. That is not—"

"It is the only way," Edward said, interrupting me.

"You cannot absolve your guilt for one murder by committing another," I said. "This is reckless. Foolish. You'll be found out."

Edward leveled the gun at my heart, one eye squinted shut. "You wandered into the middle of a firing range, cousin, and hunting accidents happen all the time. Bullets fly astray. Though, it will be especially sad for you, since you survived the explosion in Simla only to find death at the hands of your own cousin. But everyone will be sympathetic for me when I weep and mourn you. When I crumble to pieces with guilt and consider not accepting my inheritance out of shame, they will encourage me, uplift me. They will tell me it was not my fault, that you wouldn't blame me. I will accept the money, begin life again, and live every day in your memory. That is how my story will go."

"That is a fairytale, Edward," I said, replacing the scrap of paper. I tucked the locket back under my dress, and pressed my palms together, begging him to see reason. "They will wonder why you were in the woods alone, why you were shooting through densely grown trees rather than into the nye of pheasants."

"No one asks a weeping man such questions," Edward said, certain of himself.

Edward was always so confident. Convinced he was the brightest, most capable person in any room. Why would he be any different when it came to murder? He still thought himself capable of the perfect crime, yet I had discovered his secret. I was seconds away from telling him this very fact when I saw the tiniest flicker of his finger against the trigger. I dove sideways just as a deafening shot rang out.

The foliage off the path was thick, and I struggled against vines and leaves as I rolled over and got to my feet. I could hear the delicate fabric of my dress tearing as I propelled myself deeper into the forest. Edward shouted after while he reloaded, but I didn't turn back to see whether he was following me. I knew he would be.

The sun struggled to break through the dense canopy of leaves overhead, so I had some shadow to hide in, but I had cut such an obvious path through the underbrush that even the most inexperienced hunter could have tracked me. I couldn't slow down or stop running until I made it back to the others, until I could see the party and explain what was going on. Surely, Edward wouldn't shoot me in front of his family. He couldn't kill the entire group to hide his crimes. He would have to surrender and admit to what he had done.

So, I ran.

I took daily walks in London to stretch my legs and enjoy the fresh air and sunshine, but I hadn't done nearly enough physical exercise to prepare me to run for my life. My lungs felt like lead balloons in my chest, weighing me down, and my legs might have been filled with wet sand. I stopped running long enough to work up the energy to scream, but the sound was drowned out by gunfire, which didn't seem quite as far away as it had only a few minutes before. I wanted to scream again, but I could hear Edward moving through the brush behind me, gaining on me. I knew as soon as he had a clear shot, he'd take it. So, I pushed on.

When we'd first arrived at Ridgewick Hall and taken a tour of the grounds, I'd thought the woods were a little thin. Lady Ashton kept going on about the joys of being so close to nature, but I thought their "forest" seemed rather sanitized. Like a city dweller's idea of nature that a true outdoorsman would scoff at. Now, however, I felt as though I were crawling through an endless jungle. How far had I walked into the woods? Daylight felt like it should constantly be just beyond the next tree, but instead I saw only more trees, more shadows. Branches grabbed for me like greedy claws and I was constantly ripping my dress away from vines and thorns. I had stepped into a purgatory from which I would never escape.

Then, mercifully, daylight. A sob escaped my lips when I saw it between the trees. The tall grasses of the field and the bright blue sky beckoned to me, and I dug deep within myself for the strength, the endurance to reach it. It almost seemed like a mirage that would vanish by the time I got to it, but I pushed on regardless. I wouldn't die in the dark.

When I finally stepped into the grass, I stopped for a moment, blinded by the sunlight. I felt safe in the light and warmth, but then I realized no one could see me yet. The men were hunting beyond the hill, and the rest of the party was even more distant. I'd ventured further than I'd thought, so I pressed forward.

It was much easier to run across the field than the forest, but my legs were tired and burning, and my heart felt seconds away from exploding. I kept reminding myself that I just needed to reach the hill. I needed someone to see me. Anyone.

Too curious to resist any longer, I turned to see Edward stumbling out of the woods behind me. Like me, he was momentarily blinded by the sun, but he quickly adjusted. Like a falcon eyeing its prize, he narrowed his sights on me and ran, the gun resting on his shoulder. I let out a yelp and continued forward.

The hill. I just needed to get to the hill.

I pumped my arms, my dress billowing behind me in the wind. Then, I reached the crest of the hill and ran directly into a nye of pheasants. They took to the sky in a flush, swirling around me in a mess of wings and feathers and tails. I threw my arms over my face to protect myself and then, a shot cracked through the air.

I dropped to the ground out of instinct, diving away from the danger, making myself as flat as possible on the ground. I breathed and waited for the pain, for the beating in my ears to lessen as the blood flowed out of me and into the ground. Then, I heard the screaming.

I looked up just as Lord Ashton reached the top of the hill, Lady Ashton not far behind him. He looked at me for a moment, but quickly moved past me. I followed his trajectory to a dark lump at the base of the hill.

Lord Ashton fell to his knees and lifted the shape into his arms, blood flowing down his hands, and I realized it was Edward.

I heard the screaming again. Only this time, it was my own.

15

"I didn't see him on the field," Charles said for what felt like the hundredth time. He didn't seem to be capable of saying anything else. "I didn't see him. He wasn't there just a moment before I pulled the trigger. He ran directly into the path of my bullet."

"Where is Dr. Shaw?" Lord Ashton yelled in a strangled voice, paying no attention at all to anyone or anything except for Edward. He stroked his son's hair and planted a kiss on his pale face.

"He went to get his medical bag from the car," Lady Ashton said. She was next to her husband in the grass, but her glassy eyes kept darting from Edward to me. I could see the conflict in her face, the tear between loyalty and honesty. She knew why he'd been chasing me but couldn't say anything before I did without revealing she had known of Edward's guilt all along.

I took the scene in slowly, knowing I had time. I wouldn't be dying today.

Dr. Shaw came back, his usually gray face a shocking shade of red. He immediately pushed the Beckinghams away and went to work on Edward, trying to stop the blood flow. Lady Ashton continually asked whether he would live, but Dr. Shaw refused to answer.

"Will he survive? Has he died?" she asked through tears that threatened to silence her.

Mrs. Worthing and Vivian arrived while Dr. Shaw continued to work, but Lord Ashton asked Catherine to take Alice back to the house. It broke my heart to think I would have to tell the girls of their brother's sins.

"Horrible weekend," Vivian said, pounding a fist into the dirt. "None of us should have come."

I had to agree. The information the Chess Master had promised me about Jimmy suddenly didn't seem as important. Was it worth the disintegration of my family? Worth the pain Edward's death would cause the Beckinghams and Catherine? And Alice? Poor, sweet Alice who adored her older brother, despite his many faults would be devastated by what he'd done.

"What were you two doing here?" Mr. Worthing asked. "You were standing directly between our guns and the birds. Did you not see us?"

"There is no need to place blame, dear," Mrs. Worthing said. "Clearly, it was a horrible mistake, and I'm sure Rose feels terrible enough as it is."

Lady Ashton looked at me, and whether it was my imagination or not I couldn't be sure, it looked as if she gave me a slight head nod.

"Actually," I said, taking a deep, steadying breath. I still felt like I was recovering from my run across the field. My lungs burned and my legs felt weak and flimsy. "It was not an accident."

Everyone turned to me, except for Dr. Shaw who was

still working away on Edward, giving the bleeding man all
of his focus and energy.

"It was an accident that we ran into the line of fire from
the hunters, but I only crossed the field here because
Edward was chasing me."

"What do you mean he was chasing you?" Vivian asked.
Her pale blonde brows were knitted together in concern. She
had shown a serious fondness for Edward, and this news
seemed more disturbing to her than Edward being shot.

"I mean," I said, wanting to make the truth as plain as
possible to avoid needing to rehash the story multiple times.
"Edward intended to kill me in the woods. He was aiming
his gun at me, so I ran."

Vivian's face didn't change, but Mrs. Worthing threw her
hands over her mouth, stifling a loud gasp. Mr. Worthing
and Charles looked at one another and then at Edward.
Lady Ashton looked like she could be sick at any moment.
But Lord Ashton had turned an angry shade of red. His neck
seemed to be pulsing as he lifted himself to his feet.

"What are you talking about, Rose?" He spat my name at
me, his eyes wild.

I swallowed and looked down at the ground. "I was
taking a walk when I discovered Edward trying to bury
something in the woods. It was a vial that had once
contained poison. The poison he used to kill Mr. Matcham."

Mrs. Worthing gasped again, this time clutching the arm
of her husband so tightly he winced and wrenched it out of
her grip.

"But Dr. Shaw said Mr. Matcham died of a heart attack,"
Vivian said.

"Clearly, Rose is traumatized," Lord Ashton said.
"Edward was probably chasing her to warn her not to

venture into the field, and she mistook it for a threat. Someone needs to take her inside and let her calm down."

I stood up, hoping no one could see how much I was shaking. "I'm perfectly calm, Uncle, and I'm sorry to have to deliver this news, but it is the truth. Edward admitted to me that he murdered Mr. Matcham with a poison that mimics a heart attack. That was why the doctor and the authorities believed he died of natural causes."

"Why would he do such a thing?" Lord Ashton asked, though his words were more of a challenge than a genuine question. "What purpose would he have in killing a man who has been a family acquaintance for years?"

I faltered for a moment, not wanting to share Catherine's secret romance with Mr. Matcham if it was unnecessary. However, I also couldn't leave any room for doubt in the minds of the Beckinghams or their guests. They needed to believe Edward was guilty. Not only so the truth could be known, but so the Chess Master would award me my prize. It felt selfish to be thinking of such a thing when Edward was bleeding out on the grass and everyone was looking at me as though I might be mad, but I wanted the experience to at least help me on my quest to locate Jimmy and clear his name of wrongdoing.

"Edward was hoping to protect the family's reputation," I said rather cryptically.

"From what?" Lord Ashton asked. "Mr. Matcham was a scoundrel, but he had nothing to do with our family aside from living nearby."

I shook my head. "That's where you are wrong. Edward discovered a secret romance between Catherine and Mr. Matcham. He tried to ask Mr. Matcham to leave Catherine alone, but Mr. Matcham refused. So, fearing for the reputation of his sister and the family, he lured Mr. Matcham to the estate for the weekend and killed him in the night."

Lady Ashton hung her head in quiet shame, but Lord Ashton seemed to grow larger. He rumbled like the sky before a storm. "That is absurd. Absolutely absurd. There is no proof of any of this."

"There is a letter hidden in a box beneath Catherine's mattress," I said without hesitation. "It provides all the necessary proof of her connection to Mr. Matcham."

"And what proof have you of Edward's involvement, beyond your word?" Lord Ashton asked.

His disbelief stung. Even though I'd only lived with the Beckinghams for a short time, I had come to think of them as family, and I'd hoped they felt the same towards me. But it was clear, now that I was speaking out against Edward, where I fell in the family hierarchy.

I crossed the grass, and Lord Ashton stiffened, straightening his spine as though he was preparing to go toe-to-toe with me. When I walked past him, he deflated and turned. As I neared Edward, I slowed, still nervous he would regain consciousness and attempt to murder me, though it would have been far too late to save his reputation. Dr. Shaw glanced up at me as I approached, but his eyes were glazed over with focus. He was covered in blood up to his elbows, but he didn't seem to mind. His dedication to his work was commendable, and I hoped he would forgive me for briefly suspecting him of murder.

"Step away and let Dr. Shaw do his work," Lord Ashton commanded.

"I will not interfere," I said as I reached down and dug through Edward's back pocket. When I stood back up with the empty vial in my hands, everyone gasped.

"It's true," Vivian cried, shaking her head. "I cannot believe it."

"No one can," Mrs. Worthing said. "It is unthinkable. He seemed like such a good young man."

"He was...is a good man," Lord Ashton stumbled, the anger in his eyes replaced with disbelief.

Lady Ashton hadn't moved from her spot in the grass and it looked as though she never would. I walked over and sat down next to her in the grass, carefully placing my arms around her shoulders.

"I'm so sorry," I said to her. I didn't know exactly what I was apologizing for, but it felt necessary. Her life would never be the same. Her family had been unalterably changed in the space of a couple of days, and even though I hadn't set the events in motion, it was at least partially because of me.

Lady Ashton said nothing as she reached out and squeezed my hand in hers. We stayed there on the grass until Edward was carried away under the doctor's supervision, his parents trailing helplessly behind him.

16

After the weekend at Ridgewick Hall, I was more glad than ever to have a place of my own to return to. It allowed me plenty of quiet time to sit with my thoughts. And more than that, it ensured I didn't have to return home with the Beckinghams.

I hadn't dared venture over to Ashton House since returning to London, but Lady Ashton had sent me a letter, which Aseem delivered to me four days after I arrived home.

"A letter from your aunt, Miss Rose," he said, stepping into the sitting room, one hand folded behind his back, the other clutching the thick cream envelope.

I practically jumped from my chair and ran towards him in my excitement. But once the letter was in my hand, fear took hold. What would she have to say to me? Though, I knew the Beckinghams were not truly my relatives, they had come to claim that role in my life. I would miss them dearly if they never wished to see me again, though I would understand if that was their preference. Finally, once I dismissed Aseem and took a few stabilizing breaths, I slid my finger beneath the seal and opened the letter.

. . .

DEAREST ROSE,

THERE ARE NOT WORDS ENOUGH to apologize to you for the harm Edward attempted to cause you. I never imagined him capable of such cruelty. Everyone knows you are a clever girl, always watching and observing while everyone else is focused on their own dramas, and I suspect you know more about that weekend than you said at the time. For that I am grateful. Please know I will always regret my role in events. I am only glad no harm came to you.

I WILL TRY to come visit you soon.

LOVE ALWAYS,
    Aunt Eleanor

THOUGH, it was comforting to know Lady Ashton didn't blame me for what happened to Edward in Somerset— probably because she was dealing with her own guilt about knowing Edward had killed Mr. Matcham and attempting to cover it up rather than turn him in—I knew the same couldn't be said of Lord Ashton. He had been hesitant to accept his son's crimes even when faced with the evidence, and since I was the person to deliver the news, his anger had shifted towards me. I suspected that was the reason Lady Ashton said she would try to visit rather than inviting me over. I would not be a welcome face in their household for a considerable amount of time. I hadn't had opportunity to speak with Catherine or Alice to gauge their displeasure with me, but I expected their affections to have cooled at least slightly.

The day after the letter arrived, it was confirmed that Edward was fully expected to survive his gunshot wound. Things had been uncertain for a few days, but now that his survival was almost guaranteed, I knew I would be expected to testify against him at trial. A mixture of relief and terror washed through me. On one hand, I was glad my cousin was not dead, if only so his family would not have to suffer so much. On the other hand, he had murdered one man and attempted to murder me, as well. I would have slept better those first weeks back in London had I been able to rest in the fact that Edward was gone. I wouldn't have sat up in bed at night at every slight noise, wondering whether he had come to finish the job.

More than expecting Edward, however, I sat in eager expectation for the Chess Master. No matter how unconventional my method may have been, I did solve Mr. Matcham's murder and reveal the killer, which meant I would be receiving my promised reward.

When I first opened the box the Chess Master had sent, I assumed he had found me because of my previous experience investigating murders. After the attention I had recently attracted when I solved the murder of the bartender at The Chesney Ballroom, it wouldn't be difficult for someone like the Chess Master to track me down. However, now that the situation had unfolded, I had come to believe the Chess Master chose me less because of my abilities and more because of my connection to Edward.

In his confession, Edward had told me of a mysterious man to whom he owed a great debt, the same man who had provided him with the poison to end Mr. Matcham's life. I believed that to be the same man who contacted me. The mysterious man had betrayed Edward, pretending to help him by obtaining the poison, all the while ensuring I would be there to prove him guilty after the murder had taken place. It was clearly some terrible form of punishment for the money Edward still owed the criminal.

The box the Chess Master had left for me contained a pawn, and upon first receiving it, I'd taken it to be a symbol of the game I was stepping into, of the puzzle I would need to solve. Now I realized I should have taken the piece at face value. The Chess Master was assigning me a role in his game. I was to be nothing more than a pawn, a throwaway piece he could use to carry out his own plans. I hated being used as a tool, knowing I'd been tricked into carrying out his cruel "justice."

I spent many nights wondering what would have happened if I'd turned down the Chess Master's offer. Would Edward have been arrested? Would I still be dining twice per week at the Beckingham Estate, partaking in banter with Edward and listening to Alice's excited prattle about whatever she'd done that day? It was hard to say. Achilles Prideaux had suggested I stay far away from whatever plans the Chess Master had in store for me, but I now wondered whether that ever would have been possible. In some ways, it felt like I would have ended up at Ridgewick Hall that weekend regardless.

17

Days turned to a week and a week into several without any word from the Chess Master. I wanted to reach out and contact him, to send him a message of some kind, but that was hardly possible. I could not contact a ghost. I thought, perhaps, he was simply waiting for confirmation that I had solved the murder, but when articles about Edward and Mr. Matcham began appearing in the papers and still there was no word, I worried. Had it all been a trick? Did the Chess Master have any information about Jimmy or had I been fooled and used for nothing?

Lady Ashton still hadn't been to visit, though we'd written one another several times. I promised her I was staying busy, meeting with friends and remaining an active part of the London social scene—though, that was far from the truth. And she swore to me that the family was doing surprisingly well despite the circumstances. Catherine was finally coming out of her mourning for Mr. Matcham and Alice was showing a great deal of maturity in her response to the whole situation. I noticed Lady Ashton mentioned nothing of Lord Ashton in her letters, and I suspected that was because he was not dealing with things quite as well. Edward was the Beckinghams eldest child and their only son. He was meant to take over control of the family's fortune and estates one day, as well as inheriting the title, when his father passed on. But that would not be possible now.

One day, just as I was thinking of heading out to run several errands in the city, there was a knock at my front door.

"Miss Catherine is here to see you," Aseem said, walking into the sitting room ahead of my cousin, ushering her towards me, and then slipping silently away.

I stood up at once, my mouth hanging open in surprise. I didn't even manage to greet her.

"Is this how you welcome guests to your home, cousin?" Catherine asked, a shy smile playing on her lips.

I shook my head and did my best to smile. "Forgive me, Catherine. You were the last person I expected to visit me."

"I would have guessed my father would be the last person you'd expect to come here."

"Actually," I said, "I've expected your father to come and shout at me any day now. I know he must be very angry with me, and I'm sorry for that."

Catherine crossed the small distance between us and wrapped her thin arms around my shoulders. "Do not apologize. You have done nothing wrong."

I hugged her back, grateful for her kindness, and noticed how petite she felt. When she pulled back and looked down at me, I noticed the hollows of her cheeks looked deeper and there were shadows under her eyes. It was clear she was going through a difficult time, and I wondered whether it was because of her grief for Mr. Matcham or her brother. Perhaps, both.

"That is kind of you to say," I said. "I can't help but feel partly responsible for everything that is happening. I am the one who found Edward and had to deliver the news to everyone. I wouldn't blame you if you harbored ill will towards me."

Catherine shook her head, her golden hair glimmering in the light from the chandelier just above us. "Nonsense. No, Rose, you did nothing wrong. Edward tried to do to you what he did to my poor Thomas."

I placed a hand on her shoulder. "I'm sorry about that, as well. I know you were fond of Mr. Matcham."

She swallowed back her emotions, sniffling slightly. "Yes, quite fond. Unfortunately, he was a very misunderstood man. He had his faults, of course."

"Don't we all?" I added quickly, to which Catherine smiled.

"Yes, absolutely. He was not a perfect man, but I, as I'm sure you already know, am hardly a perfect woman. Regardless of what Edward says, I believe Thomas loved me very much. We were planning to marry soon. Once we'd made all the proper announcements to our families, of course." She looked down at the floor, her eyes losing focus, as though she were deep within a memory. Then, just as quickly, she pulled herself out of it and gave me a somber smile. "But plans change."

I offered to let her stop and sit for a moment, but she declined.

"I'll only be here a moment. Mother and father will be expecting me home soon. I just wanted to come and see you."

"I'm so glad you did," I said. "I have missed you."

Catherine squeezed my fingers, and then her posture changed. She seemed to be making herself smaller, as though she didn't want to be seen, which was very unlike Catherine. The entire time I'd known her, she swelled under the smallest bit of attention. She'd mentioned her own faults only a few moments before, and one of hers was vanity. Much like her brother felt certain he was the cleverest person in any room, Catherine was convinced she was the most beautiful. So, seeing her bow her head and stoop her shoulders was an unusual sight, to say the least.

"After everything you've been through these past few weeks, I hate to come and ask anything of you. Especially since this is the first time I've seen you since that dreadful weekend in the country," Catherine said, puckering her face at the thought of our time in Somerset.

"Don't be silly," I said. "Ask me anything."

Catherine took a deep breath, and then rushed through her next words as though she couldn't say them fast enough. "I know Edward confessed his crimes to you, and I know he threatened to harm you, but I hope you know how absolutely out of his head he was that weekend. If he had been thinking clearly, I don't believe he would have sought to do you any harm. You are family, after all. A most beloved cousin to all of us."

I wanted to argue that I didn't believe Edward would ever describe me as a most beloved cousin, but I was much too focused on what Catherine would say next.

"I just want you to consider your testimony against him," she said, her eyes pinning me to the spot. She was staring at me as though she wanted to see through me, as though we could communicate via thoughts rather than words.

I nodded slowly. "I am considering it very carefully."

This was true, though not what I suspected Catherine

meant. Because my life had been threatened, part of me wanted to lay out everything to the courts. I wanted them to know how heartless Edward had been. How remorselessly he had talked about ending my life and how easy he believed it would be to convince everyone it had been an accident. Edward had revealed himself to be almost sociopathic However, there remained another part of me that wanted to protect my family from the cruelty of one of their own. I didn't want them to hear the horrible things he'd said, how heartless he'd been. It could destroy them.

Catherine looked at me with a slight disappointment in her eyes. She didn't think I understood what she meant, but I understood perfectly. She didn't want me to testify.

"I just don't want you to go through the trauma of reliving that day if you don't think it would add anything to the case," she said with a simple shrug, as if what she was suggesting had almost no importance.

"He killed your would-be husband," I said. "You said yourself that he would have killed me."

She shook her head. "Maybe. But we can't know that for certain."

"He aimed and fired directly at me. The only reason I wasn't struck is because I dove out of the way and ran," I said, my frustration barely concealed. "He chased me halfway across the sprawling property. If he did not wish to kill me, then I cannot imagine what it is he planned to do with his weapon."

Catherine took a step back, her lips tightening. "I know my brother."

"And I know how it feels to be threatened with a deadly weapon," I said. "This was my third time, and I've become closely acquainted with the signs. I am terribly sorry for the loss you and your family are going through. I understand how it feels to have a family member accused of a horrible crime. However, do not think for a moment that I will withhold the truth to spare the man who tried to kill me. He is my cousin, and I wish there could be another outcome, but I am afraid he has given me no choice. I hope you will all find it in your hearts to forgive me for doing what I must."

Her eyes became hard and focused like marbles. "You've never had a person you care about convicted of murder," she said quietly. "I realize what Edward has done, but he is my brother, and I do not wish to see him hang or spend the rest of his life behind bars."

I realized then that I had slipped. Catherine knew nothing of my brother Jimmy, of the crime he had been accused. She couldn't know any of that if she was to believe in me as Rose. So, rather than insist that I did understand exactly how she felt, I pinched my lips closed and nodded in agreement.

"But," Catherine continued, already half-turned towards the door. "I also cannot deny you your justice. I only came to offer up my opinion. I hope you know that I will support whichever decision you make."

Catherine left with few other words uttered between us, and I couldn't help but doubt her unswaying support. I knew if I testified against Edward that things could and likely would be different between us, but that couldn't stop me from telling the truth.

I tried to take up the book I'd been reading before Catherine's arrival, but my thoughts wouldn't settle. I felt restless and the house suddenly felt too small. So, throwing a cream-colored sweater over my shoulders and tucking my hair into a navy cloche hat, I took off out the front door with no particular destination in mind.

Since the weekend in the countryside, I hadn't gone

walking nearly as often. Not only had the activity lost some of its allure, but I stayed close to home in hopes that the Chess Master would find me and deliver the reward he'd promised. But now, that was the last thing on my mind. I simply needed to breathe some fresh air and see something aside from the four walls of my home.

The sun was halfway through its descent across the sky when I'd left, but before I knew it, I was in a part of town I didn't recognize, and the sun was almost hidden beyond the horizon. I'd been walking for hours. I'd walked through the afternoon, through dinner, and into dusk. My feet were tired, so I turned back for home, but still my mind ran with thoughts of seeing Edward in court, sitting on the opposite side of the room from the rest of the Beckinghams. My real parents had been murdered, Rose and her parents—the closest thing I'd had to family for most of my life—had been murdered, and then the family I had found in London might be torn away from me because of another killing. It felt as though I'd been cursed.

The sidewalk I was on narrowed and curved between two buildings. I remembered walking that way before, but it had been lighter then. Now, with the sun setting, the road appeared to be no wider than an alley and it was plunged in darkness.

I pulled my sweater tighter around my shoulders and quickened my pace. The road was empty now, most everyone having retired to their homes for the evening. I was halfway through the alley when I heard a scuffling noise like feet against stone. I wondered whether it wasn't the echo of my own feet, so I stopped. Still, I heard it.

My heart leapt into my throat as I began walking again, trying to remain calm. I thought that perhaps I was simply paranoid. Being attacked three different times by murderers could have that kind of affect on a person. But then, the steps grew louder. My head swiveled from side to side, my eyes searching the darkness for any kind of movement.

"Who is there?" I called, my voice hesitant and fearful even to my own ears.

No one answered, and a chill ran down my spine. It felt as if someone was walking directly behind me, their breath brushing down my neck, yet I couldn't find them. I knew I wasn't alone in the alley, but there was nothing I could do except keep walking and hope the person wouldn't reveal themselves. So, I lowered my head and pressed on, my feet beating out a quick rhythm against the stone walkway.

I was nearing the end of the alley, the last remnants of daylight brightening the road ahead, when a figure rushed me from the side. By the time I saw them, I could do little more than hold up my hands and back into the brick wall next to me. The figure threw a bag over my head and flung something into my arms. Then, they were gone.

18

I struggled with the sack over my head for a moment, frantically pulling and tugging at the material to free myself, and once I had it off, I stood stiff and straight against the wall. My chest heaved with fear and adrenaline, and my eyes darted up and down the street, expectant, but no one came. No one attacked me further.

I realized that the person must have placed the sack over my face to hide their own identity. They were not there to attack me, but to deliver a message. Finally convinced whoever had placed the bag over my head was gone, I looked down at the plain brown box in my arms. It felt impossibly light, and I wondered whether it wasn't empty. I was tempted to open it on the street but decided against it. If the package was, as I suspected, from The Chess Master, it would be better to open it in the privacy of my own home. Especially if it had something to do with Jimmy or my search for him.

The box weighed almost nothing, but it felt heavy as I carried it all the way across the city and back to my house. I regretted walking as far as I had because it took the better part of an hour to get home, even though I followed a more direct route than I had earlier.

"I was worried about you, Miss Rose," Aseem said when I finally returned. "Dinner was ready an hour ago. Should I reheat it for you?"

"I am not hungry tonight. Thank you, Aseem."

The boy looked at the box in my hands but didn't say anything. Instead, he nodded and disappeared into the kitchen. He was a loyal servant who asked very few questions, and I was grateful for him.

I went to my bedroom and set the box on my bed, taking a step back to observe it. Was it the information I'd been waiting for? The box was the same type and shape as the last box the Chess Master had left for me, so I had to assume it was. I'd been waiting to hear from him for so long that I hadn't stopped to think about what kind of information he might offer. What if it wasn't what I wanted to hear? What if I opened it and discovered Jimmy was dead? Or that he could never be found? What would I do then?

I paced back and forth several times, trying to convince myself to open the box. I wouldn't know what the information was until I opened it, and until I opened it, I would be able to think of nothing else.

Finally, before fear could stop me, I took a deep breath and slipped a small knife through the wrappings that held the box together. I pushed the lid off slowly and peered inside. What I saw sent my heart thundering against my chest.

The box had felt nearly empty as I'd carried it across the city, and now I understood why. Inside was nothing except for one faded piece of paper with a hastily written message on it. The note was yellowed with age and a narrow strip had been torn from its edge, interrupting the written message. The handwriting scrawled across the paper was familiar.

Without even thinking, I opened the locket around my neck and pulled out the note I'd carried with me since I was a child. The note that had propelled me from India to London. That had led me to assume a new identity and claim an inheritance that was not mine. The note that had convinced me of my brother's innocence in the murder of our parents, that had given me faith in him and helped me believe he couldn't have done what the police and public had accused him of.

The tiny scrap was so old it was a wonder it didn't crumble in my hands as I unfurled it. The scratchy handwriting was more familiar to me than my own. I'd spent countless hours studying the note, wishing I could talk to my brother, wishing I could know the circumstances under which he'd written the plea: "help me."

I smoothed the two words out and placed the uneven scrap of paper perfectly against the torn edge of the note I'd just received. A sob tore through me as I leaned over the box, reading the full message for the first time. It had never occurred to me that I'd only found a part of Jimmy's message, that there had been more to the sentence. But now, faced with the truth, I felt sick.

"God help me, I killed them."

My entire life had been based on the note I'd carried in my locket. Everything I'd done had been to locate Jimmy, to offer him the help I'd been unable to at the time I'd found the note. Now, what did any of it mean? What did my life mean if it had all been based on a lie? Or, rather, an absence of the full information?

I'd always thought Jimmy needed my help. It made sense, too. He was always a sensitive boy, more easily frightened and overwhelmed than other children. Even though he was older than me, I was the one who stood up for him to neighborhood bullies when we were kids, who took the blame when one of us was going to get into trouble. Imagining that same boy killing both of our parents seemed beyond impossible. What motive could he have had?

My thoughts turned back to that horrible day a decade ago when, as a child of thirteen, I had come home to my family's New York apartment and stepped inside the doorway. In my mind's eye, I sped past the horror of finding the bodies of my murdered parents. The details rushed past in an indistinct blur. I didn't let myself dwell on the gory scene. Instead, I focused on the tiny scrap of white, the strip of paper that had lain on the floor near the door. It commanded my attention now as it had then, something safe to keep me from seeing and feeling the shocking things around me.

I had knelt in the floor, numb to everything except the puzzle of that little slip of paper: the words "help me" scrawled in my brother's handwriting. I shut out everything else, letting the message assume enormous importance. Jimmy wasn't there in the apartment. He had been there when I had gone outside to play earlier, but now he was gone. Where was he?

It was a question that would occupy my mind, giving me a much-needed source of distraction and a purpose for years to come. When the police began the search for him later, I knew he was innocent. And every day until I'd opened the box the stranger had handed me in the alley, I'd known Jimmy was innocent.

Now, I was filled with nothing but doubt.

19

E dward didn't matter to me anymore. Not really. The conversation with Catherine, my relationship with the Beckinghams, anything that had to do with me being Rose Beckingham didn't matter to me. I only had room in my mind for thoughts of Jimmy. Of my old life in New York City. Of the fateful day that had brought everything crashing down around me.

Over the years, I'd created a narrative of what I thought happened. I'd built up the idea that perhaps Jimmy had walked in on the killer and had run away in fear, returning later to leave me a message so I'd know he didn't do it. Or maybe he had stumbled upon the dead bodies of our parents and had known he would be blamed for the crime, so he'd dropped the note in front of the door and ran before anyone else could find them.

No matter what scenario I created in my mind, Jimmy, the older brother I had loved and cherished all my life, was innocent. Always and forever innocent. Now, I couldn't be sure.

For the first time, I could see the other possibilities. I

could see Jimmy holding the bloody murder weapon. I could see him grabbing his things and fleeing the scene before I returned. I could see him hiding from the authorities and anyone who might recognize him for the next nine years.

I still couldn't see the motive, though. No matter how long I stared at the two matching puzzle pieces of the note, I couldn't understand why Jimmy would do such a thing. The last time I saw him, he'd been smiling. He'd given me a small wave. That boy wasn't a murderer. Not when I'd left him, at least. What could have changed?

I moved the pieces of paper to my desk and then picked up the box again, studying it for any hidden clue or message, but there was nothing. Then, the idea came to me. Like Edward, was I falling for a trick? Was the Chess Master making a cruel game out of my life? I couldn't begin to understand how it could be possible, how he could have forged the second part of a note my brother had written so many years before or mimicked his handwriting so precisely. But I also didn't understand how he had found me miles away from my home in order to deliver the box. I didn't understand many things about the Chess Master, but that had no bearing on his abilities.

I rotated the box in my hands again, frustration and heartbreak rising up in a wave I couldn't keep back. Suddenly, I hurled the box across the room. It smashed against the back of the stone fireplace and then fell into the white log below in a shower of embers. The fire flared around the new kindling and then died down just as quickly. I wanted to drop the note into the flames, as well. Let the fire cleanse the world and my mind of the information that was written there. But I couldn't do it.

What if it was true? What if Jimmy really had killed our

parents? I couldn't throw away the evidence, and I could no longer hold on to the small piece of paper I'd carried with me for so long. Not now that I knew it could be part of the longer message. Everything had changed and burning the note wouldn't scrub the knowledge from my mind.

I'd hoped the Chess Master would give me information on Jimmy's whereabouts. That he would help me find my brother, so I could finally ask him what had happened that day. Now, though, I was left with more questions that I'd started with and no way to contact the Chess Master to answer them.

As I flopped down into the chair in the corner of my room, the note as far away as possible on the desk in the opposite corner, I had a thought. It was true I couldn't contact the Chess Master, but maybe he wasn't the only person who could help me.

Knowing sleep wouldn't come, I settled in for a long night of waiting. Because in the morning, I would be going to see Monsieur Achilles Prideaux.

I LEFT JUST as the sun rose, reminding me of my early days in London when I'd had to sneak out of the Beckingham's home before they awoke. The morning was crisp and dewy. Water droplets colored the leaves silver in the morning light and the stone sidewalks glistened. Fog like smoke hung over the horizon, making the world feel closed in and small. I took a deep breath of the damp, fresh air, but all I could smell was New York.

The sights and smells from the explosion in India had haunted me the past few months, but now a different murder scene was coming back to me. The one I'd seen in the home I shared with my parents and brother. And to think my brother could have been the culprit? My stomach roiled and flipped.

Thankfully, Monsieur Prideaux lived only a short walk away. Now that the Beckinghams were less inclined to visit me, it was nice to know I had someone resembling a friend living close by.

Monsieur Prideaux's landlady lived directly above the detective and was shaking out a small rug when I arrived. Debris and dust floated from her window in a great cloud, and I stood back, hand held over my eyes until she finished.

"If you're here about the room, it's already claimed," she said, rolling the rug into a tube and then leaning through the frame on her elbows. "But it can become unclaimed for the right price."

"I'm not here about the room," I said. "We've actually met before."

The woman's face didn't change as she stared down at me.

"I'm here for Monsieur Prideaux," I explained.

Her face sagged down into disappointment. "Then, why are you wasting my time?" She disappeared back through her window and slammed the pane closed before I could answer.

As I walked up the three stairs that separated Achilles' porch from the sidewalk, his door opened. It had been a few weeks since I'd seen him—the last time having been when I'd brought him the first box I'd received from the Chess Master—and it was easy to forget how handsome he was. Although, he didn't go anywhere without his cane, which I knew actually disguised a small blade to be used as a weapon, and refused to shave the thin black mustache just above his lip, he was still a good looking man. Tall and lean, a crop of inky black hair on top of his head, and a deep tan to his skin. He wore a gray suit and waistcoat, a gold pocket watch chain dangling from his inside pocket to his waist, and a light gray derby hat.

Although he had been on his way out, he showed no sign of disappointment at having to delay his plans.

"I wondered when I'd be seeing you again, Mademoiselle Beckingham," he said, turning sideways and ushering me inside, using his cane to point towards the sitting room.

I stepped into the cool, well-lit space of his entryway. "Please, Monsieur Prideaux. I believe we have spent time enough together for you to call me Rose."

"Mademoiselle Rose, perhaps," he said, closing the door behind him. "Can I interest you in any tea? I also have juice and coffee, if you'd rather."

"No, thank you. I'm fine," I said. I'd already had several cups of tea that morning and my hands were jittery with sleeplessness and nerves. "But by all means, I can wait if you'd like to get yourself something."

He seemed to consider it for a moment, his lips pursing, and then shook his head. "No, I'm much too interested in what could have brought you to my doorstep so early in the morning after weeks with no contact."

"You are more than free to contact me at my house," I said with a coy smile. In the presence of Achilles, it was almost easy to forget the stress I'd been under for the last twenty-four hours.

"I did not wish to disturb you," he said, his face growing suddenly serious. He ran his finger along his mustache and then pressed it to his lips. "I know your family has been faced with a difficult time of late."

I nodded, trying to remember when the fate of Edward

and the Beckinghams had been the most upsetting thing in my life. "So, you've seen the papers, then?"

"I'm afraid so. Are you confident Edward is Mr. Matcham's killer?" he asked. "I knew Thomas Matcham casually, and he had a rather close connection with the Beckingham family. With the eldest daughter, in particular."

"You know of their secret affair?" I asked, eyebrows raised in shock.

"I did not know it was a secret," he said with a shrug. "Mr. Matcham always made time to see Catherine when he was in town, and he spoke very highly of her. His affections were plain to see. If it was a secret, it was poorly kept."

"Perhaps it was poorly kept for a world-renowned detective," I said with a smile. "Because it was quite a shock to the rest of the family. Edward seemed to be the only one who knew about it."

"And he did not react very favorably." Achilles shook his head. Then, his eyes narrowed on me. "Would it be rude of me to mention that I warned you not to become involved in any more danger?"

"It wouldn't be rude at all. You made a suggestion and I chose to do otherwise. As long as neither of us is bitter about the series of events, then I see no reason why it should matter," I said.

The truth was, I didn't want to talk about it. Achilles had been right about staying away from trouble. If I hadn't gone to the countryside that weekend, not only would Mr. Matcham's death likely have been ruled a natural one and the Beckinghams wouldn't be faced with sitting through a murder trial for Edward, but I wouldn't have solved the case and the Chess Master never would have delivered the alleged second half of Jimmy's note. Life would have continued on as it had, and even though it would have been a lie, I wouldn't have known the difference.

Achilles gestured for me to take a chair in front of his fire and then claimed the matching chair next to it as his own. "Me, bitter?" he scoffed and waved me away. "Never. I should have expected nothing less from you. I'm not sure if you have made this connection yet, Mademoiselle Rose, but you have a penchant for getting yourself into trouble. In fact, you seem to run headlong into it."

"Has it ever crossed your mind that perhaps trouble has a way of finding me rather than the other way around?" I asked.

He smiled, his white teeth glimmering like smooth stones. "Never."

I eased back into the comfortable chair, soaking in the yellow light in the room and the glow coming from the low fire. Achilles stood up to stoke it slightly, pushing a log back, embers swirling up in a small funnel before settling again. It felt nice to be with another person. The weeks after Somerset had been lonely, though I hadn't realized it until I was sitting in Achilles Prideaux's sitting room.

"The papers made little mention of it, but I suspect you are responsible for your cousin being behind bars?" Achilles asked.

"And why would you suspect that?"

He raised a thick brow at me and tilted his head down. "I believe your history answers that question for me. Would this not be the third murder you have solved? If I'm not careful, there may be another famous detective living in this neighborhood."

I folded my hands in my lap. "To be honest, I stumbled upon the truth quite by accident."

"You would be amazed how many cases are solved in

exactly that same way," Achilles said. "You are more of a detective than you think."

He was smiling, but I sensed a coldness behind his words. Could Achilles Prideaux really be worried about me stealing some of his work? I didn't know, and that wasn't why I'd come to see him.

I waved him away and readjusted in the chair, sitting up straighter. "I've done nothing but talk about Edward for days. I've come to speak of something else."

"I'm surprised anything else could even compete for your attention. In fact, most everyone I know is speaking of the Ashton heir and his fall from grace."

"I'm sure you remember the box I received just before the weekend in Somerset?" I asked.

He nodded. "The chess piece and the note, yes. Did the anonymous sender reach out to you again?"

I swallowed back my nerves. "He did. Last night."

"He? So, you saw him?" Achilles asked, leaning forward, his elbows resting on his knees.

"No, not exactly. In fact, I don't believe the sender makes his own deliveries. I was accosted in an alleyway, blinded, and the box was thrust into my hands. By the time I removed the blind, the person had run off into the night."

"What were you doing in an alleyway at night?" Achilles asked, reaching out to grasp my wrist, his eyes wide and sincere.

I patted his hand twice before he pulled it away. "Are you worried for me, Achilles?"

He stood up and moved quickly to stoke the fire in the fireplace again. "I just want to know you are being careful."

"Always," I said, though we both knew it was a lie. When he reclaimed his seat, I continued. "I know I have already asked you to help me locate the man named Jimmy, but I would like your assistance in locating the sender of the boxes, as well."

"I have been looking into the matter of the boxes, though I haven't discovered anything yet."

"I know. I just wanted to make it an official inquiry. This is no longer a friend coming to another friend for help. Consider me a client. I want to pay you to find the Chess Master for me."

"The Chess Master?" his brows pulled together.

I flushed slightly. "It is a moniker I've given him because of the chess piece left in the first box. It is a substitute for his name. Once you are able to discover his true identity, I will gladly call him that, instead."

He nodded, his face contemplative. Finally, he sighed and looked up at me. "Of course, I will assist you, Mademoiselle Rose. Whoever this person is, they clearly know a great deal about you, and for your own safety, it would be better if you could know something about them in return."

I nodded in agreement, not telling Achilles exactly how much the Chess Master knew about me. From his first letter, it had been obvious he knew my secret identity. That information could be very powerful in the wrong hands, and I had a strong feeling that the Chess Master's hands were, indeed, wrong.

"So, what was in the box you received last night?" Achilles asked. "Did you bring it with you?"

Again, my face warmed with embarrassment. "I'm afraid I no longer have the box."

"Why not? What happened to it? That is important evidence."

I, again, decided it would be best not to tell him that I'd thrown the box into the fire in a fit of frustration. He didn't need to know how deep of a connection I felt to what I was about to show him.

"I do have what was inside the box, though," I said, reaching into my clutch and pulling out the two pieces of paper. They were scarcely the size of my palm when put together.

"'God help me, I've killed them.'" Achilles read the note slowly. He picked up the smaller piece and then re-fitted it against the larger note. "Do you recognize this handwriting?"

I shook my head. I still wanted Achilles to help me find Jimmy, and it would be best if he didn't know the person I wanted him to find was likely a double murderer. That information might make him unwilling to help me any further. And also, I needed to protect my own identity. No matter how much information he found out about Jimmy or even Nellie, I couldn't allow him to know I was not Rose Beckingham.

"So, there is nothing else you can tell me about the man who sent you these?" he asked.

I thought back, trying to recall anything even slightly incriminating, but there was nothing. "The only thing I know is that the sender has people working for him. The man who accosted me last night was not the same man I saw standing beneath my window several weeks ago. They had very different builds. Either one of them was the Chess Master or the Chess Master is more important than we think and has many underlings."

"As I said before, if the man knows of a murder before it is committed, we must assume he has a connection to the criminal world. In which case, it is possible he has followers," Achilles said.

"I agree. Edward mentioned reaching out to a man for

the poison he used to kill Thomas Matcham. I believe the person who supplied that poison is the same man who is contacting me. Or, if not, I at least believe the two men are connected."

"I tend to agree," Achilles said, his lips puckered. "I fear you may have somehow found yourself involved with some very serious criminals."

"Does that information make you not want to help me?" I asked. "Because I would understand if you don't want to be involved."

I was offering Achilles Prideaux a way out, but I hoped he wouldn't take it. The truth was, without him, I would have a difficult time finding any information. I'd been placing so much hope in the Chess Master for the where-abouts of Jimmy, but the note he'd delivered did nothing to help me find Jimmy. All it did was ruin the image I'd culti-vated of my brother over the years. It cast a long shadow of doubt over everything I thought to be true.

"Mademoiselle Rose, if you think I am afraid of a few amateur criminals, then I beg you to get to know me a little better. I will not be backing down from your case, and I hope to return to you with news in the next few weeks."

"Thank you, Achilles. You are one of the only people I can trust these days."

He placed his hand on mine briefly and smiled. "We will speak again soon, Rose. I hope to have more information to offer."

On my walk home, the sun had begun to rise in the sky, burning off the fog and dew of the morning. People filled the sidewalks and streets, going about their daily business. Except now, I studied everyone with a suspicious air. Were they simply strangers going about their business? Or, were they associates of the Chess Master watching my every move? Despite what Achilles had said about the Chess Master being an amateur criminal, I couldn't help but think he was downplaying the man's skills. The Chess Master had enough contacts to know when far away murders were being committed and when pretend-heiresses were masquerading under false identities. He had underlings to do his bidding and had somehow managed to find the second part of a note that had been written nearly a decade before.

Though the morning was warm, I shuddered, a panicky chill rolling down my spine. Far from being an amateur, I believed Achilles and I were searching for a criminal mastermind.

20

I filled the following days as best I could. There was still much unpacking to be done, which Aseem and I set to with quiet diligence. He carried boxes for me, making no complaint despite his small size, and I filled my home with the scant decorations I'd managed to accumulate. Through her letters, Lady Ashton had offered many things from her own storage and I'd gone shopping for the others, visiting local stores for candle holders and picture frames to fill the walls. Slowly but surely, the home I'd bought for myself was becoming an actual home. Not simply a cover story for my disguise, but a place I really wanted to spend my time in.

If Aseem noticed my lack of visitors and how infrequently I was leaving the house, he didn't mention it. I assumed he and George had both read the papers. They likely knew what had happened with Edward in Somerset, and noticed that I hadn't been going to the Beckinghams for dinner, but neither of them asked me any questions. It was nice to have a place where I wasn't forced to consider the fate of Edward, my tenuous relationship with the Beckinghams, and the identity of the Chess Master. I could focus on interior decorating and whether picture frames were straight on the walls. It was a safe haven.

One week after Catherine's impromptu visit and after I'd received the second package from the Chess Master, there was another unexpected knock on my door.

"Miss Alice Beckingham, Miss Rose." Aseem waved Alice into my sitting room and then made himself scarce, closing the double doors behind him.

"Alice," I said, crossing the room quickly and wrapping my arms around my youngest cousin. I hadn't realized how much I'd missed her until she was standing in front of me. I hadn't seen her since the day Edward had been shot, and it had been many weeks since then. "What are you doing here?"

She hugged me back, which was a relief. I didn't know how much she knew about what had happened with Edward or my role in it. If she knew everything, I would not have been surprised to find her reluctant to talk to me, let alone hug me.

"It's good to see you, Rose." Her voice was measured and even, far from her usual giddiness. Though, there had likely been very little happening in her life that would cause giddiness.

She wore a pale violet tea dress that swung loose around her blossoming hips and a low-heeled pair of Mary Janes. Her long brown hair was pinned into a swirl at the base of her neck and covered with a felt hat with a large felt bow on the side. As much as I wanted to pretend Alice was a little girl, she was turning into a woman. It seemed as if she had aged five years in the last few weeks.

"What are you doing here?" I asked again, grabbing her

hand and pulling her to the two-seated sofa in front of the fireplace. "Does anyone know you are here?"

"They all left to visit Edward this morning but told me I couldn't come." Her lower lip trembled with annoyance and frustration. Beneath her womanly appearance was still the little girl who begged to be included. It was almost a comfort to see a glimmer of the Alice I had come to know.

"Do you really want to see him?" I asked, trying to be gentle. "In that place?"

"Is he in a real prison?" she asked, eyes wide. "With bars on the doors and slop for food?"

I couldn't say for certain what kind of prison cell Edward was in, but I had to assume it wasn't glamorous. It definitely was not the place for a fifteen-year-old girl. "I'm not sure of the conditions, but it isn't a place you'd want to visit. It's full of the worst kinds of criminals."

Her eyes flashed for a second, and I realized what I'd said. I opened my mouth to take it back, but Alice lifted a hand. "It's all right. I know what you meant. I just have a hard time thinking of Edward that way."

I nodded, not sure what to say. I didn't want to tell her anything her parents didn't want her to know. I wasn't sure what Lord and Lady Ashton would do if they knew I'd welcomed her into my home and then shared the whole terrible truth with her.

"You can stop looking so nervous," Alice said, a tender smile spreading across her pink lips. "I know everything."

I narrowed my eyes at her. "Everything?"

"Everyone likes to think I'm a silly girl who doesn't know what is going on, but I pay attention," she said, jutting her chin out. "I know Edward killed Mr. Matcham, I know Mr. Matcham and Catherine were a couple, and I know Edward tried to kill you."

"What are you doing here?" I asked for the third time.

"I wanted to see you," she finally said, her shoulders sagging. "It has been weeks and you haven't been by the house."

I grabbed her hand in both of mine and squeezed. "I'm not sure anyone wants to see me right now."

"I do," she said, nodding firmly. "And so does Mama. I know she does."

I tilted my head to the side. "But your father? And Catherine?"

She rolled her eyes. "Papa is always visiting Edward and Catherine never leaves her room. She has been wandering around the house dressed in black. She claims it is because of Edward, but I know it's for Matcham. I can hear her crying through the wall that separates our rooms. I didn't even know they were in love, and now she is mourning him. It is so strange."

Alice was talking fast, the words getting jumbled as they tumbled out of her mouth. She spoke as though she'd been dying to talk for weeks but hadn't had the opportunity. And it was likely she hadn't. Everyone seemed to always be a little short with Alice, so now that they were especially busy and sensitive, they probably weren't very interested in what she had to say.

"It's normal to be sad," I said, trying to defend Catherine. "She cared about Matcham."

"Not enough to tell us about him," Alice said, clearly bitter her sister had kept a secret from her. "And I can't even imagine what Edward was thinking. It seems impossible that he could have done such a thing."

I grimaced and then nodded. Even after Edward had confessed, I found myself reluctant to believe him. Edward had a good family and a solid position in life. It was unthinkable that he could have thrown everything away in the name of his family's reputation.

"How did everything become so terrible?" Alice asked, tears collecting in her eyes. "Edward and I played croquet in the grass the day after he..." she let the sentence trail off, not wanting to say what he had done.

I patted her back, rubbing my palm in circles over her sharp shoulder blades.

"That was such a good day. I thought we were having so much fun, and now I see it all differently," she said.

"I understand," I said, wishing I could tell Alice how much I really did understand her. I could completely relate. The letter I'd received from the Chess Master had brought into doubt all of my memories of Jimmy. If he really had killed our parents, how long had he been planning it? A few days? A week? Or had it been a spur of the moment decision? And if so, would he have killed me too had I not been out of the house? Suddenly, our entire relationship felt suspect. Just moments before opening the box, I would have sworn Jimmy loved our parents fiercely, but now I didn't know, which meant I didn't know anything about him.

Alice smiled at me, though it didn't reach her eyes and I could tell she was unconvinced. "I came here because I heard Papa and Catherine talking."

"If it isn't something they intended for me to know, then I'm not sure you should—"

"I know Catherine came to see you," she said, interrupting me. "And I know she asked you not to testify against Edward, but I wanted to come and tell you that I want you to do whatever you feel is right."

I leaned back and looked at her. "You don't mind if I stand in front of the court and tell everything that happened? Even if it means Edward never comes home?"

She swallowed hard, tucked her lips to the side of her mouth, and then shook her head. "If Edward really did what everyone says he did, the world should know it."

I wanted to squeeze Alice. I wanted to hold her to my chest and cry and tell her over and over again how thankful I was for her. For weeks I had felt like I was facing off against the Beckinghams, like I was the one tearing their family apart, but Alice had brought an entirely new perspective. Edward had committed his crimes. Not me. Being honest about the things he'd done wouldn't transfer his blame to me. I would always be the victim, and he would always be the culprit. Nothing would change that.

"That's a very grown up thing to say, Alice," I finally said, my throat thick with unshed tears. "I appreciate you coming to see me very much."

She smiled, but when the clock above the fireplace chimed, she looked at it and her smile disappeared. "I should get back. They don't know I left the house, and I'd like to keep it that way."

I walked her to the front door, my hand on her back. "I'm not sure when I'll see you again," I said, deciding it was best to be honest with her.

"Soon, I'm sure," she said. "Everyone will have to calm down eventually."

"I'm not sure if that's true. But I hope you are right," I said. "I'd love to join you all for dinner again soon."

"I'll mention it casually to Mama," she said. And then, when she noticed the worry in my eyes, she added, "Do not worry, I'll be very subtle about it."

Alice adjusted her hat over her ears and opened the front door. However, once she reached the top step she turned back to me, her eyes sad and thoughtful. "Do you think it is all right to still love him?" she asked. "Edward, I mean? Do you think it is wrong to love him even after every-thing he has done?"

I could tell Alice was ashamed to ask the question. Espe-cially of me, of all people. Her brother had tried to kill me and, had he not been shot himself, likely would have succeeded. However, I could also see the struggle behind the question. I could see how much thought she had put into it. So, I gave her as honest an answer as I could.

"Love is rarely simple. And it certainly isn't sensible. There are no rules, so if you love Edward despite what he has done, then you should feel free to feel that. You do not have to explain yourself to me or anyone else. He is your brother, and though he did something horrible, he is still your brother. It's all right to love him."

I didn't realize until after I'd finished speaking that tears were streaming down my face. Alice threw her arms around my waist and buried her head against my chest.

"Thank you, Rose," she said. "I needed to hear you say that."

I hugged her back and realized that I had needed to hear it, too.

21

I received a letter from Mr. and Mrs. Worthing the day after Alice's visit. The letter was four pages long—mostly to do with what Mrs. Worthing described as their "horrible" train ride back to London after our weekend in the country—but the final page caught my attention.

I CAN'T HELP but feel partly responsible for your current heartache. Not that either myself or Mr. Worthing had anything to do with Mr. Matcham. But because we swore in India to see you safely to London, and it seems as though you have been anything but. Trouble seems drawn to you for some reason, Rose, and I wish more than anything I could draw it away. That isn't possible, of course, but please know that our door is open to you anytime.

SENDING OUR LOVE,
    Mrs. Worthing

. . .

I TUCKED the letter into the drawer of my desk on top of the stack of letters I had collected from Mrs. Worthing since arriving in London. Mostly, she spoke about herself, which fit well with what I knew about her as a person. But occasionally, as in her latest letter, she showed some concern for me and my wellbeing, which was comforting.

I hadn't heard anything from Achilles Prideaux in over a week, and I was growing anxious. With little else to occupy my time, it was hard not to dwell on the possible crimes of my brother or the identity of the Chess Master. I saw and heard him everywhere. In every creak of my floorboards, in every bump in the darkness. I knew paranoia was creeping over me, but I couldn't stop myself. He knew everything about me, and though I knew next to nothing about him, the one thing I did know was that the Chess Master was not the kind of person to give up an advantage. He knew my true identity, and it was only a matter of time before he decided to use it against me.

The sun had only just set, but it was already dark outside my window. Dark gray clouds covered up the moon, plunging the street below into dark shadow.

I stood at my window, my robe pulled tightly around my middle, preparing to tuck into bed with a book, when I saw a movement just beyond the wrought iron fence that circled my property. It was in the exact same place where the Chess Master had first left me a package. I squinted, focusing my eyes on the shadows outside the halo of light from the streetlamp, when suddenly a figure stepped into view.

I jumped away from the window with a yelp before regaining my composure. The figure was dressed in dark clothes with a hat pulled low over his eyes. I couldn't be sure, but it looked to be the same man who had stood outside my window before. The man who had brought news of the murder that would occur in the countryside, who had started my life down its current path.

The first time he'd stood there, I'd waited by my window in fear, not daring to go down and confront him. Now, however, I didn't have time for fear. There wasn't room in my brain for anything other than unanswered questions. So, without hesitating, I spun on the spot, hurled my bedroom door open, and took off down the stairs.

Aseem would no doubt hear me running through the house and come to see what was wrong, but I couldn't worry about that now. I had to get outside and stop the man before he could escape again. I needed to see his face, see whether I knew him. Or, at the very least, have a good description to give to Achilles Prideaux.

I slid and nearly fell going down the stairs in my slippers, but I caught myself on the banister and used it to propel me into the entrance hall. I unbolted the front door and threw it open, leaping down all three stairs in one jump.

My chest was heaving with exertion, trying desperately to take in air, but even still, when I reached the gate and saw the empty spot where the man had been standing, my heart sank. I'd missed him.

I spun in a circle just to make sure, checking for any other moving shadows around the yard, but there was nothing. I was alone and breathless.

I turned to go back into the house when something caught my eye. Sitting in the center of the circle of light from the streetlamp was what appeared to be a small figurine. I opened my gate with a metal squeal and knelt down on the pavement, afraid to touch the object for a few seconds.

There could be no mistaking its meaning.

First, the Chess Master had given me a pawn, which I'd

learned over the course of the weekend in Somerset was meant to represent my role in his game. But now, knowing I was searching for his true identity, the Chess Master wanted me to know his role in our game.

On the pavement where the mysterious man had stood only a moment before, there was now a single chess piece —a king.

～

Continue following the mysterious adventures of Rose Beckingham in
"A Grim Game."

EXCERPT

FROM "A GRIM GAME: A ROSE BECKINGHAM MURDER MYSTERY, BOOK 4."

The morning was drenched in gray. Rain squelched from the heavy sky like it was being wrung out over the city and fallen leaves mildewed along the streets and sidewalks. Everyone who found themselves out in the dreary day kept their heads down, hats pulled low over their eyes, shoulders hunched near their ears. It felt like the perfect day to visit prison.

I'd debated a long while about whether I wanted to visit my cousin Edward in prison or not. He was set to stand trial for the murder of Mr. Matcham, along with a charge of attempted murder for when he tried to kill me, as well. The last time I'd seen my cousin, he'd fired his gun at me and chased me halfway across his family's large property in Somerset before being accidentally shot himself. So, given the circumstances, my desire to see him again was minimal. My curiosity, however, drove me to make the trip.

Before he attempted to murder me, Edward had made his confession. He'd told me that he contacted a powerful man in London's criminal underworld to obtain the lethal and rare poison he'd used to kill Mr. Matcham. I had reason to believe the man Edward spoke of was the same man who had written me prior to Mr. Matcham's demise to warn me of a death in the countryside. The man I had come to refer to as the "Chess Master" due to his penchant for leaving chess pieces along with his notes. And after his latest delivery of the most powerful chess piece on the board, the King, I could no longer keep my burning questions to myself. Edward had seen the Chess Master's face. He had done business with him before, and I knew he could tell me the mysterious man's true identity.

The Surrey House of Correction, where Edward had been moved since recovering from his gunshot wound, was a good distance from my home. While I had my own personal driver, George, I didn't want him to know of my plan. He wouldn't have been able to stop me from visiting Edward, even though he would have wanted to, but still, I wanted to go alone. I didn't want to have to explain to anyone why I was visiting my attempted murderer. And I especially didn't want to have to explain it to the rest of Edward's family. So, I took a cab and instructed the driver to drop me off a distance from the prison, opting to walk the rest of the way. The Beckingham family was understandably shocked and appalled by Edward's actions, and as the trial loomed, they were trying to keep a low profile. The last thing they needed was for news of my visit to reach the papers—*Edward Beckingham's Victim Turned Visitor*.

There had been enough articles in the last few weeks about the "divide" Edward's crimes had caused. Not only had he murdered his sister's secret lover—an affair which was no longer secret—but he had attempted to murder me, his own cousin. Reporters claimed to have the inside story, explaining that I was at odds with the Beckinghams, and that they would never forgive me for taking the witness stand to testify against their son and brother.

None of it was true, of course. True, Catherine had come to me and asked that I consider not testifying against Edward, and Lord Ashton had been reluctant to accept that Edward could truly be responsible for the crimes he was charged with. But, as time had gone on and the investigation came to a close, the truth had come out, and no one could deny Edward's guilt. After weeks of not seeing the Beckinghams, I'd received an invitation to dinner, which I'd readily and nervously accepted. There, the family had sought to make amends.

"We are so glad you accepted our invitation," Lady Ashton said, reaching out to grab my hand and squeeze my fingers. "We all missed you, Rose."

I smiled at my aunt and then cautiously glanced around the table. Alice was nodding in eager agreement with her mother, and I was relieved to see that Catherine and Lord Ashton were nodding, as well.

"I missed you, as well. All of you," I said, giving Catherine a pointed look. She smiled.

Lord Ashton coughed, his fist over his mouth, and then began to speak. "When all of this came to light, things were confusing. We didn't have all the information, and it was impossible to think a family member we all loved could be capable of such a horrific act. In our desire to clear Edward of blame, I know it may have felt as though some that blame landed on you, Rose."

I shook my head, trying to stop Lord Ashton's apology in its tracks. I had been hurt by his anger towards me at first, but soon I came to realize from where the feelings stemmed. It was easier to blame me than to think he had raised a murderer. And while it wasn't fair, I understood. I didn't blame him for anything he'd said or done in those confusing days.

"No, it's important that this is spoken aloud and made known. We are all sorry for any additional pain we may have caused you, Rose. As the truth has been revealed, we have come to accept Edward's responsibility. And in doing so, have been ashamed by how you were treated and abandoned in the early days of the investigation."

Lady Ashton hiccupped, and I looked over to realize she was crying. I patted her shoulder, and she covered my hand with her own, her lips pursed in a sad smile.

Lord Ashton continued. "You are a prized member of this family, Rose. Edward sought to harm you because of his own guilt, and he has brought shame on our family. His crimes will forever be a blight on our honor. But you, dear Rose, represent the best the Beckinghams have to offer. We asked you here to dinner, so we could formally apologize to you for our behavior in the days and weeks after the murder."

While the declaration had been awkward and left me nearly speechless, it was nice to hear, nonetheless. The Beckinghams were the closest thing to family I had left—I highly suspected Lord Ashton would not have made such an apology to me if he knew I was not truly Rose Beckingham, but actually her former servant in disguise—and I wasn't eager to lose them anytime soon.

Still, even with the apology, it was difficult to be around the family of late. While they had forgiven me, they still struggled to accept Edward's new identity as a murderer, and my presence and the impending trial did little to help them forget. I did my best to keep my distance and offer them privacy to mourn and come to terms with their new reality. And that meant I had no intention of telling them about the visit I was paying to Edward in prison.

The sun was rising behind the massive brick building, casting it into deep shadow. It looked like a blot on the horizon—a black ink stain across a perfectly clean sheet of paper that should be crumpled up and forgotten. Even looking at the building from the outside was a dreary exercise, so I didn't particularly wish to experience the inside. However, that would be the only way to speak with Edward.

The guards at the gate were reluctant to let me inside, but the men inside were even more difficult to convince. One of them, a balding man with a thick mustache and dirty suspenders, crossed his arms where he stood behind a cluttered desk and shook his head when I asked to see Edward Beckingham.

"He's on trial for murder. Only family allowed," he barked, dismissing me with a wave of his hand.

"I am family," I said.

He raised an eyebrow. "You a sister or something?"

"Or something." I didn't want word of my visit to make it back to the Beckinghams, and I didn't want anyone to look at me the way so many people were looking at me lately, with pity in their eyes. I had survived and I had my freedom. As far as I was concerned, I was not a victim, though it was difficult to convince everyone else of that.

The man shifted his weight from side to side, stretching his shoulders out wide. "You can't see him unless you are blood family."

I sighed. "I'm his cousin."

He narrowed his eyes at me. I could see the ghost of recognition in his face. "Cousin?"

"Do you know anything about this case?" I asked.

The man nodded his head slowly, clearly suspicious of

me. I couldn't exactly blame him. He probably didn't see many young women knocking on the prison doors before sunrise, a hat and scarf pulled around their face to avoid detection.

I unwound the thick scarf from around my neck and draped it over my arm. "I'm Edward's cousin. *The* cousin."

His overgrown brow furrowed for a second and then jolted upward in surprise. He shook his head as he pushed the door open and let me inside. "That makes you family, all right."

I was directed to a small concrete room to wait. It smelled wet and stale, and I found it difficult to inhale. For a moment, I felt a twinge of sympathy for Edward. He was accustomed to a much more luxurious life than what prison offered. And just as quickly as my sympathy came on, it passed. Edward was a murderer. A man who would have murdered again to save his own hide.

Just as I had this revelation, the door opened and a pale, thin creature was thrown in the room with me. It took several seconds for me to recognize my cousin. In the weeks he'd been in prison, his face had hollowed, his tan skin had turned an ashen gray color, and the thick dark locks of his hair had gone dry and brittle. Still, there was a familiar spark in his eyes, a haughtiness that couldn't be tempered by incarceration.

"Hello, Rose," Edward said, tipping his head to the side as if he needed to see me from another angle to be certain it was me.

"Edward." I tried to keep my voice level, unemotional. If I showed any weakness, he would latch onto it. I had to be unaffected if I wanted to gather any information from him.

He lowered himself into the wooden chair across from mine, moving slower than I'd ever seen him move, though he had the same graceful air. "I didn't expect to see you until the trial."

"I didn't expect to come," I admitted.

"And why did you?" he asked, leaning back, hands folded over his chest. It was then I noticed the metal cuffs around his wrists, the chain that bound them together. It was a comforting reminder. He could not hurt me here. Just outside the door was a guard who would burst into the room at the first sign of trouble. "Surely, you've been told not to fraternize with me. I suspect you'll be testifying against me in the trial."

It was a statement more than a question, but regardless, I had no intention of responding to it.

"I'm not here about the trial, and I don't intend to discuss it with you. The decision regarding my testimony is my own." I paused, leveling my gaze at him so he would know I was serious. Then, I continued. "I'm here to ask you a question."

Edward's dark eyebrows rose slowly. "Ask whatever you'd like, dear cousin. I cannot promise an answer, but I can promise to listen."

Dear cousin. The words sounded slimy rolling off his tongue, and suddenly I wanted to take back the entire idea. Instead of sitting across from Edward in prison, I wanted to be warm beneath the blankets of my bed at home. I swallowed back my rising nausea and looked Edward square in the face.

"You mentioned the shadowy figure who supplied the poison you used to end Mr. Matcham's life," I said, easing into the question.

Edward shook his head. "I said no such thing."

I furrowed my brow, confused. And then Edward winked, and I realized what was going on. He wouldn't be heard by anyone—me or the guard—admitting to his crimes.

"You mentioned a member of the criminal underworld," I said, rephrasing the question. "Would you tell me his name?"

"Why are you interested in associating with a criminal?" he asked. "I thought you were the solver of crimes, not the purveyor of them."

The truth was, I didn't want to seek out the Chess Master at all. I wanted to forget about him and move on from the entire incident. However, I'd asked Detective Achilles Prideaux to look into the whereabouts of my long-lost brother Jimmy—though Achilles did not know our familial connection—and he hadn't had any luck. Whereas, the Chess Master had supplied me with solid evidence that he had some connection to Jimmy, though I had no idea how strong it was. He was the only person who had given me any hope of finding my brother, yet I had no clue as to his identity. Unfortunately, the Chess Master knew my secret identity. He knew I was not truly Rose Beckingham but actually Nellie Dennet, and I knew he could choose to share this information anytime he wanted. It felt as though an invisible sword was held just above my head, and with every passing day, the blade lowered. I had to find the Chess Master as soon as possible.

And as it stood, Edward was the only person I knew who could connect me to the Chess Master, and the Chess Master was the only person I knew who could connect me to Jimmy. Essentially, Edward was my only hope.

I knew, however, that I couldn't tell any of this to Edward. He was in a precarious legal situation, no doubt facing terrible punishment should he be convicted of murder, and my testimony would almost certainly convict him. If he knew how desperately I needed this information, he would definitely try to use it as a bargaining chip, and then the only way I'd get anything out of him would be to choose not to testify or to lie on the witness stand.

I said, "The man has sought me out on several occasions but has kept his identity a secret from me. I would like to know to whom I have been talking."

"He contacted you?" Edward asked, dubious. "Why would he do that?"

"It is not important," I said firmly. "Can you help me uncover his identity or not?"

Edward lifted his chin, looking down his nose at me. "Of course, I can. The question is whether I will or not."

I sighed and stood to leave. "This is ridiculous. I am not here to play games with you, Edward."

"You aren't going anywhere," Edward said with a laugh.

He was right. He'd called my bluff. I had no intention of leaving the cold, damp room until I had an answer one way or the other from him.

"You may be surprised to hear this, Rose, but the men in here are not excellent company. So, you'll have to excuse me if I drag this meeting out awhile longer."

"Why do you want to talk to me?" I asked. "You tried to kill me, remember?"

Edward shook his head, a small smile on his lips. "I did no such thing. Though, if I had, it surely would have been out of necessity and not because of any ill will towards you."

A shiver ran down my spine. Why hadn't I ever noticed Edward's cool manners? The way he spoke around the truth, dangled the true meaning of his words in front of you like a treat and then yanked them back? He was diabolical. Though, I reminded myself, he was also in prison. He'd been fooled once—by me, in fact—and he could be fooled again. As always, he believed himself to be the cleverest person in the room, but one of us could leave the cage, the other couldn't. Clearly, I had the upper hand.

"Actually, I will leave. I don't want the information badly enough to endure this horrid place," I said, pushing my chair back and smoothing out the chiffon fabric of my dress. "I'll be sure to send my regards with your family, whenever they are able to make it out for another visit. If not, I'm sure I'll see you in the courtroom."

Edward's face was expressionless and stony as I left the table, but by the time I was halfway to the door, he cracked.

"Wait," he said, swiveling in his chair, the chains around his wrists clanking on the table. "I will give you answers."

I stopped, one foot lifted mid-step, and looked over my shoulder. "I told you. I don't want answers badly enough to spend any more time here. You want to toy with me, Edward, and I'm not interested."

"The roof leaks in my cell," Edward said, his voice quiet, wavering around the words. "It's cold and damp. Men die in here because of the conditions. I've felt ill for weeks. Even if they don't execute me, I'll die in this place."

I turned to face him, my arms hanging loosely at my sides. I had never seen Edward look so vulnerable. Still, I didn't want to give him even the tiniest hint that I felt for him.

He lowered his face, staring down at his feet, and continued. "I wanted to protect my sister's honor—my family's honor—but instead I have besmirched it irreparably. The only thing I ask is that you all do not forget me."

His words echoed off the hard walls until everything aside from our breathing went quiet. Then, a metallic bang rang out, and I instinctively ducked.

"Visit over," the guard outside the door barked, not even bothering to form a full sentence.

Edward looked up at me, eyes wide, stricken. "Come back," he demanded. "Come see me again, and I'll tell you whatever you want to know."

The guard banged on the metal door again, and I moved towards him, my ears ringing.

"Please, Rose," Edward called, outright begging now. "Come see me again. I'll help you with whatever you need. Please."

The guard opened the door for me and I stepped into the hall. Just before the door closed, I gave Edward one small nod. His face broke into a hopeful smile, and then the door slammed closed, and he was gone.

END OF EXCERPT

ABOUT THE AUTHOR

Blythe Baker is a thirty-something bottle redhead from the South Central part of the country. When she's not slinging words and creating new worlds and characters, she's acting as chauffeur to her children and head groomer to her household of beloved pets.

Blythe enjoys long walks with her dog on sweaty days, grubbing in her flower garden, cooking, and ruthlessly de-cluttering her overcrowded home. She also likes binge-watching mystery shows on TV and burying herself in books about murder.

To learn more about Blythe, visit her website and sign up for her newsletter at www.blythebaker.com